GREEN SKY AT NIGHT

BOOK ONE OF THE GREEN SKY SERIES

JENNAE VALE

CHAPTER 1

Giant sea swells smashed against the side of the ship as Danielle York made her way up on deck. She needed air and the last thing she wanted was to be stuck below deck at the party she was hosting along with her best friend and business partner, Susanna Cole. Escaping the confines of the ballroom was the only thing on her mind, other than questioning her choice of venues for Sanders and Ash's annual summer bash. This was by far one of the riskiest corporate events she'd put together and the fact that she was feeling a little green around the gills proved her point.

"Danielle, are you okay?" Susanna, a petite brunette, hurried to follow her.

Another wave hit the ship and Danielle grabbed onto the rail to keep from losing her footing. Susanna was at her side, holding her arm.

"Tell me again why we chose a fantasy pirate ship party for this event?" The world swirled around her as she focused her eyes on the horizon fighting to keep down the hors d'oeuvres she'd eaten earlier.

Susanna looked her in the eyes. "This was a great idea," she assured her friend. "Who knew you'd be prone to seasickness?" She carefully examined Danielle with a mix of what could only be described as pity and concern.

"What?" Danielle managed to squeak out. "I haven't been on a boat in ages. I'd forgotten how much I hated it."

"Too late now." Susanna's raised eyebrow and pursed lips said it all.

Sounds from the party taking place below deck wafted up to them.

"One of us should go back down there and make sure everything continues to go well. By one of us, I mean you." Danielle gripped the ship's rail as if her life depended on it.

"Are you sure you'll be okay?" Susanna touched her arm, her voice filled with concern.

"No, but it's nothing I can't deal with. Go. I'll be back down as soon as I can." She leaned heavily on the rail. If she had to barf, this was the place to be. No one else was around to witness her embarrassment.

"I'm going to get you something to help with the nausea and a nice glass of ginger ale. I'll be back in a few." Susanna did a crab-walk sideways to the stairs leading down to the ballroom as she fought the rolling of the ship.

Danielle and Susanna had been friends since junior high and were now business partners whose sole mission was to plan the best corporate events around New York State. They were lauded by former party goers and their business had picked up incredibly over the past few months. This pirate cruise had been her idea. She'd pitched it to the people who mattered at Sanders and Ash, an up-and-coming real estate brokerage firm, as a fun cruise to Bermuda aboard a modern-day pirate ship. Costumed crew members gave the adventure an authentic feel. Some of the guests even got into the spirit by wearing eye patches, swords and tricorn caps.

The weather had been beautiful and the seas calm. Danielle hadn't experienced any ill effects from the voyage until tonight when the ocean decided it'd had enough of them. It was the last night they'd be at sea, docking tomorrow morning in Bermuda where the party would continue, and then they'd thankfully be boarding a plane to return home to New York at the end of the week.

Lifting her head and gulping in the fresh salt air drifting on the breeze, she decided to make her way to the back of the boat. What did they call that? Was it aft? She knew next to nothing about boats and really didn't care to. This would be her last voyage, of that she was sure.

Rounding the deck, she arrived at her destination. The crystal clear sky put the full moon on display. It was beautiful and she would have appreciated it a whole lot more if she didn't feel quite so ill. Much to her delight, the ocean seemed to be calming. The ship wasn't listing from side to side anymore. Maybe it was done and she'd manage to make it to Bermuda without getting sick. Relieved, she leaned against the rail of the ship and, as she did, she noticed that the sky appeared to have gone from deep, dark blue to an odd shade of green, which moved across the horizon and in front of the moon causing it to glow liked a colored lantern hung high in the sky.

Danielle had to share this with Susanna. She thought briefly about heading back down to the party to find her, but since she was starting to feel better, thought it a good idea to stay where she was and wait for her friend to return. The odd color of the sky reminded her of the colorful Northern Lights she'd seen once on a trip to Iceland, but they were too far south to be experiencing anything like that.

A thunderous boom sounded off in the distance. There was no sign of what had caused it or where it was coming from, but the sound continued to reverberate in the night air, getting louder and louder as it closed in on her. It hit the boat, physically rocking it back. Danielle grabbed for a handhold on the rail, losing her footing and toppling head-over-heels overboard. As she sailed toward the water below, she heard Susanna's terrified shriek, "Dani!"

The next thing she knew, the water engulfed her. She fought, kicking her legs as hard as she could to get back to the surface. It seemed like forever before she broke free of the water and gulped some much needed air into her lungs. Once her eyes were back in focus, she kicked her legs and spun in place just like those synchronized swimmers she'd seen on television. To her shock and horror the ship she'd been on just moments before was nowhere in sight. She was alone in the middle of the ocean. It couldn't possibly be. The boat had been right there. Susanna saw her go overboard. Surely they'd come back to look for her.

A million things ran through her brain as she did her best not to panic. There was no room to feel sorry for herself. Danielle thought about all those swimming lessons she'd taken a few years back. She'd never learned to swim as a child. It wasn't until her friends and family suggested it might be a good idea for her to learn just in case, that she decided she should. And now floating in these dark waters, she was glad she'd listened to them and taken those lessons. One invaluable tool she'd learned came to mind. She could do a dead man's float, or a survival float as it was also known, but first she had to get out of the dress she'd been wearing. Heavy with water, it was weighing her down. She struggled with it, sinking beneath the water several times before she managed to undo the zipper and strip the sodden fabric off. Free of the extra weight, Danielle sucked in a deep breath, filling her lungs with air and then floated face down in the water, trying not to think about things like sharks or how far it was to the bottom. If her swim instructors were right, she should be able to safely do this for hours, which she wouldn't need to because the ship would be back for her by then.

Pulling her head out of the water for what seemed like the thousandth time, Danielle noted that the sky was no longer green. In fact, the sun was beginning to rise into a clear blue sky. Off in the distance, a ship appeared. She would have cried with relief, but was too exhausted. Waiting for the boat to get closer, she frantically waved her arms in the air before thinking better of it. It seemed they'd seen her and were headed her way. She'd be saved in no time.

"Oh!" Something brushed up against her legs causing her to stop thrashing around abruptly. Whatever it was didn't seem to be visible to her and she hoped it was nothing more than the dress she'd removed earlier. The last thing she wanted before being rescued was to attract the unwanted attention of fish with sharp teeth. "Hurry, hurry, hurry," she muttered through chattering teeth.

"Cap'n, there's something afloat in the water off the port side." The deckhand scrambled down from the crow's nest and made his way to Jameson Mackall, captain of *The Dagger*, handing him a spyglass.

Jameson accepted it and, placing it to his eye, searched the waters for whatever it was that his man had spied. At first, he saw nothing, but then his eye caught a glimpse of something bobbing up and down between the swells. He wasn't quite sure what it could be, but when a head popped up from the water, he realized it was a person.

"How did they get there?" he asked, puzzled by the sight.

"Sir?" The deckhand waited for his orders.

"Not a ship in sight," Jameson said.

"Must've fallen overboard," the deckhand said.

"Jordy, tell Lynk to get as close as we can. Have the men ready the skiff to retrieve whoever it is as quickly as possible."

"Aye, sir." The man hurried away toward the helmsman with his orders.

They were miles from shore and there were only so many ways someone would end up fighting for their life in the middle of the sea. Either they were thrown overboard, they fell, or their ship sank and they were the only survivor. Jameson would know soon enough as his ship headed at top speed toward the figure still bobbing up and down. He was hopeful they would be reached before drowning or being devoured by sharks.

As *The Dagger* approached, the skiff was lowered and Jameson watched Hawes, Lynk and Jones board and row toward the figure who had once again disappeared beneath the waves.

Three men rowed frantically toward her. Danielle lifted her head as high as possible in order to be seen. She reached an arm up to wave as the rowboat came alongside her, one of the men grabbing her arms and hauling her aboard.

"Thank you," she sputtered. "I thought I was going to drown."

"'Tis a lass," the man who'd pulled her aboard noted.

"How'd ye end up in the water?" the man at the back of the boat asked.

"I fell overboard and when I came up for air, the boat I was on had disappeared."

The three men exchanged worried glances.

The man who'd pulled her aboard, seemed to be the one in charge. "Back to the ship, lads."

"Aye, sir."

Danielle took a good look at her rescuers. They were dressed in pirate garb, much like the revelers aboard her cruise ship had been. What were the chances she'd be rescued by another pirate cruise?

Thankful to be out of the water and grateful to these men, Danielle couldn't speak. Her words of thanks seemed too little to express how good it was to be alive. She shivered, wrapping her arms around her bare midriff feeling chilled.

The man who'd pulled her aboard wrapped a blanket around her shoulders. "Here, Miss, ye should cover yerself."

"Thank you," she squeaked out. A weak smile was all she could manage as she pulled the blanket tightly around herself. From her seat in the center of the boat, Danielle observed they were approaching a much grander pirate ship than the one she'd been on. *I'll have to get a brochure for future reference,* she thought. Although chances of her ever planning another cruise for her clients seemed unlikely after what she'd just been through.

CHAPTER 2

anielle knew she looked like quite the sight and the expressions of amusement from the men on deck made it clear that it might be even worse than she thought. She did her best to brush the strands of soaking wet hair from in front of her face while still trying and failing to hold the blanket close around herself.

"Take her to my cabin." A handsome, black-haired man wearing a dark blue velvet coat and tan breeches and who appeared to be the ship's captain gazed at her with an unreadable expression.

"Aye, sir." The man grabbed her arm and started leading her away.

"Gently," the man admonished. "She'll need dry clothes. Find something for her."

The crew member led Danielle up some stairs to another deck, where he opened a door for her. She entered a cabin that was authentically ornate in nature and very masculine in feel. There was a large desk covered with maps and other items she thought must be antiques or very good replicas. The large bank of windows behind it gave a panoramic view of the ocean all the way to the horizon. Unlike the ship she'd been on, this one seemed completely powered by the wind. There was no sound of a motor humming in the background.

"Sit," the man commanded.

"What's your name?" she asked, thinking if she engaged him in conversation, he might lighten up a bit.

"Hawes, ma'am. I be the captain's first mate." He gave her a slight bow before turning toward a large wooden armoire.

"This is all very authentic," she noted, glancing around the room. "Do you do party cruises?"

"Party cruises?" Hawes seemed confused by her question.

"I get it. You're supposed to stay in character. No worries. I won't tell." She gave him a conspiratorial wink before leaning back against the desk.

He scrunched his eyebrows and shook his head as he opened the wardrobe, pulled out a dress, looked at it and then at her. "This should fit ye."

Danielle accepted the dress, which was a royal blue taffeta. It looked like a ball gown. "Thank you. This is beautiful."

"I'll leave ye, miss. The captain will check in on ye soon. If ye wish to rest…" As he left, he pointed to a bed atop a built-in set of cabinets surrounded by white bed curtains. He closed the door behind him, leaving Danielle alone.

She shook thoughts of what might have happened out of her head, relieved that her ordeal was now over. Danielle removed the under-clothes she still had on and not knowing what to do with them, plopped them in a pile on the floor where water immediately began to form a puddle around them. Completely naked now, a chill passed through her and she quickly found what seemed like a man's shirt. It would have to pass for a towel. She dried herself off before donning the dress, which was impossible to fasten. She twisted herself into a pretzel pulling on the laces, but to no avail. It would have to stay open until someone could help her with it. Squeezing her hair with the same shirt-turned-towel she got as much of the water out as possible. A hot shower would be just what she needed, but there didn't seem to be a bathroom in the cabin. She'd ask the captain when he arrived. A small mirror inside the wardrobe door told her she was a mess, but there was nothing she could do about it, and really, she didn't care. She was just happy to be out of the water and alive.

Wandering the cabin, Danielle yawned. She hadn't slept since the night before last and she was starting to feel it. All the adrenaline that had been coursing through her for the last several hours was gone, leaving her limp like a wet dishrag. She sat on the edge of the bed. It wouldn't hurt to take a short nap.

"How's our guest?" Jameson asked when Hawes reappeared.

"I'm thinkin' she swallowed a bit too much sea water. She seems daft. Talking about costumes and party cruises." He shook his head. "I gave her one of yer lady's dresses."

He waited for a reply, but Jameson had nothing to say about it and after a brief moment the man seemed to get the message and walked away.

Jameson watched him go before striding across the deck and staring off to the horizon. How on earth had she ended up in the sea? The question troubled him.

"You appear bothered." Edward Sutherland's voice came from behind him. "No sign of the Spanish galleon we seek?"

"Nay. We'll find her." They'd been searching this same stretch of ocean for over a week now with no sight of the *Barco de Oro*.

"I see we've a new passenger." Edward was notoriously inquisitive about all things female.

Jameson turned to look at him. "'Tis what's puzzling me. Why was she alone in the middle of the ocean?"

"Only she knows the answer to that question." Edward leaned one elbow on the ship's rail as he seemed to scan the deck.

"True. I'll give her time to rest before I seek my answers."

"'Tis good of you. 'Tis not yer usual way with prisoners who find themselves aboard *The Dagger*."

"The lass is no' a prisoner."

"No' yet, but perhaps soon." Edward winked at him.

Jameson gazed at his old friend, who was now his quartermaster, with a mix of irritation and resignation. He knew exactly what he meant, but chose not to engage with him. Sutherland liked to get under his skin and they usually took part in a verbal joust of sorts, each trying to outdo the other. "If ye're searching for an argument, ye will no' get one this day."

"I'm disappointed." Sutherland feigned sadness, with what Jameson noted to be a pathetic attempt to draw him in.

"Don't be. I'm sure I can oblige ye at a later time." His tone was dismissive.

Edward seemed to understand that this wasn't the time to poke the beast. "What of the galleon?"

"I'll chart a new course." He turned and walked away toward his cabin. He had questions for the lass and hopefully she had answers.

Opening the door to his cabin, he spied the woman lying on his bed wearing Lady Abigail's dress. The one she'd left behind on the day he'd safely delivered her to Charleston to meet the man she was to marry. He hadn't prepared himself for the sight, nor had he expected to see the woman's bare back. She was lucky it was he who entered. Any other man aboard may have taken advantage of the lass. He cleared his throat to let her know he was there.

She spun toward him and sat up on hearing him. "Oh! You startled me!"

"I beg yer pardon, lass. I should have knocked, but I'm no' in the habit of doing so before entering my own cabin."

She awkwardly rose from the bed, the unlaced dress impeding her ability to stand. "I…" She couldn't seem to get the words out. Poor thing. She'd had a frightening ordeal.

"May I help?" he asked, not waiting for an answer. He spun her around and laced the dress as quickly as his fingers would allow, trying not to think of the other times he'd laced or unlaced this dress.

"Thank you. I've never worn a dress like this before." She ran her hands down the front in seeming appreciation of the fine fabric.

"I'm Captain Jameson Mackall. This is my ship, *The Dagger*."

"I'm Danielle York. My friends call me Dani. Pleased to meet you."

He gazed at the hand she'd put out in front of him and chose to ignore it. "Danielle, how did ye come to be floating in the middle of nowhere?"

Seemingly perturbed by his question, or perhaps by the fact that he'd chosen not to take her hand, she replied, "Good question. I wish I knew what happened. If I did, I'd be happy to share that information with you."

"Ye doona ken how ye got in the water?" His brow furrowed as he stared into her eyes and noted the confusion there.

"I do, but I don't know what happened." She fidgeted with the dress yet again.

"How can that be? Did someone throw ye overboard?" Getting to the bottom of this might not be as simple as he'd expected.

"No." She shook her head.

"Did yer ship sink?" How was it that she had no answers for him?

"I don't know." Her shoulders raised and lowered as did her eyes.

She was a puzzling lass. How could she not know?

"Danielle…"

"You can call me Dani," she interrupted.

"Danielle, I need answers."

"Or Danielle if you prefer," she said under her breath.

"Where have ye come from?" He preferred the sound of her full name and decided that was what he would call her.

"I'm from New York." She seemed to be regaining some semblance of confidence, because she straightened and, tipping her head, gave him a look that told him he might be pushing too hard.

"Would it be possible to get more than these brief answers yer giving me? I'll no' be able to help ye, if ye doona."

"You're Scottish! I love your accent by the way." She looked him over from head to toe.

For the first time since he'd met her, he really saw her. He'd been so focused on finding out what had happened to her that he hadn't noticed her beautiful sapphire eyes, slender nose and lips that while full were still a purplish color from being in the water for what must have been some time. It was hard to tell her hair color, because it was still quite wet, but it could possibly be blonde. "I was on a pirate cruise from New York to Bermuda."

Pirate cruise? Hawes was right. There was something off about the lass. He pulled a blanket from the bed and threw it around her shoulders. "Please, sit." He indicated a chair by his desk.

"I don't know why I'm so cold." Danielle wrapped herself completely with the blanket.

"The water will do that. 'Tis warm, but the longer ye spend in it, the colder yer body becomes."

"Hypothermia," she replied.

He ignored her comment. "How long were ye in the water?"

"Well, the party was going full tilt and I wasn't feeling well. I think it was about two a.m. I went up on deck to get some air. Then the weirdest thing happened. Did you see the sky last night? It was the strangest color green."

"Aye. I saw it." He'd thought it strange as well, but he'd heard tales of this from others.

"Did you hear the loud boom?"

He'd heard nothing and shook his head.

"Well, it rocked our boat and the next thing I knew I was in the water and my ship had disappeared."

He paced back and forth, fingers brushing the stubble on his chin. "'Tis a mysterious place. I've heard tell of ships disappearing here, although I've never seen it myself."

"Are we in the Bermuda Triangle? That must be it." A panicked look came over her. "Susanna!"

"Calm yerself, lass. I'm sure yer ship is still here somewhere. Who is Susanna?" he asked.

"My friend. She's still onboard. I thought they'd come back for me. Where could they have gone?" She sounded more and more hysterical.

He took her hand in his. It was icy cold, so he rubbed some life back into it. "What is the ship's name?"

"*Neptune's Gold.*"

"I'm no' familiar with it. Who's the captain?" Jameson liked to believe that he knew the name of every pirate ship that plied the waters of this part of the ocean, so he was disturbed to hear that there may be a new ship in the area.

"Joshua Jacobs."

"Never heard of him."

"We were cruising to Bermuda. It was our last night at sea." As she explained, he could see she was becoming more and more upset.

Seeing her anxiety, he felt a need to calm her fears. "We'll sail to Bermuda then. Perhaps we'll find them there." He was sure the ship had sunk, but he kept that thought to himself. The best he could do was take her to port and get her back on dry land where she might be able to find someone to help her get back home.

"You'd do that for me?" She seemed delighted. "I don't even know where you were headed. I hope it won't take you too far out of your way."

"Doona trouble yerself. We're in search of another ship. Bermuda may be just the place to find both vessels."

Feeling more at ease, Danielle wasn't above flirting with a handsome man and this one was just her type. Dark hair, dark eyes and that pirate getup he was wearing was hot. When he'd done up her laces, the feel of his fingers on her back had warmed her from the inside out. He was all business, though. So far, he hadn't given her any hint that he found her attractive. His interest had been all about the specifics of her accidental dunking. That wasn't about to stop her.

"I love your cabin. The maps, the decor. Did you design it?"

His eyebrows scrunched together as he looked at her. "Of course no."

She'd struck a nerve. Not what she was going for. She walked around his desk and lifted a paperweight from atop the maps. "The company you work for then?"

"I'm my own man." He approached the desk. "Put that down, please."

This wasn't going very well. He obviously wasn't interested. "What does your wife think of your job?"

Again, the eyebrows collided. "I'm no' married."

That was good news. She put the paperweight back where she'd found it and joined him on the other side of the desk. "This is a great ship. How many cruises do you do a year?" Those eyebrows refused to relax. She placed the tip of her index finger on them. "You're going to wear those out."

He gently grabbed her hand and removed it. "I doona understand ye, lass. Ye make no sense."

She'd gone too far. Maybe she should just keep her hands to herself. "I'm sorry. You all take this pirate thing very seriously. You don't have to, though. I'm a corporate party planner. I get it. You want to keep up the mystique for the customers, but you don't have to do that for me."

His scowl was pirate perfect. "Again, I doona ken yer meaning."

She smiled. He was very good at this. "Okay. I give up. You do you."

"I must return to the deck. Doona touch anything," he ordered.

"Do I have to stay here? Can't I come with you?"

He held up his hand. "We'll be in port tomorrow morning. For yer own safety, it would be best if ye did no' venture out onto the deck. I will sleep with my men."

"Wait. Do you have a shower? Where's the bathroom?"

"There's a chamber pot beside the bed."

And he was out the door. She'd successfully chased the man away. "I'm so out of practice." She turned away from the door that had just been closed in her face and went back to the bench by the windows where she sat with her arms wrapped around her knees. It wasn't easy with the voluminous dress she wore. She wished she had her own clothes to wear, or at the very least that her underthings were dry, but that wasn't likely to happen before they got to Bermuda. Susanna must be freaked out. Danielle felt terrible not being able to get in touch with her to let her know that she was okay, but this ship took the whole pirate thing to a new level. Imagine having to use a chamber pot. No shower. No electricity.

And no air conditioning. They apparently wanted to give their guests a very real experience. She definitely would not be asking for a brochure.

Danielle rested her head against the glass and yawned. She was exhausted and in desperate need of sleep. It didn't appear that the captain would be back, so she forced herself up and across the room to the bed where she would try once again to sleep. It wasn't the most comfortable mattress she'd ever slept on, but it would do. She was so tired she doubted she'd even notice it once she was asleep.

Her eyes popped open at the sounds of feet stomping across the deck. "Land ho!" one of the men yelled. For a brief moment she couldn't remember where she was and when it hit her, she shook her head in disbelief. It hadn't been a dream at all. Instead she realized that the terrible nightmare she'd had was very real.

The door flew open and she sat up, startled by the suddenness of it.

"Ye're awake." Jameson Mackall strolled in, looking even better to her this morning than he had last night. "Ye slept well, I hope."

"I did. Thank you." She did her best to straighten her hair, which she was sure looked like a hornet's nest now that it was dry.

"How are ye this morn?" He stood beside the bed gazing down at her. Was that concern on his face? Or maybe she looked worse than she thought.

"A little lost." It was all she could manage to get out.

"Perhaps no' for long. We're docking in Bermuda. St. George's. Yer ship should be here."

"I hope so." It had to be. If it wasn't, it only meant one of two things. Either the ship sank with everyone on board, or they'd left without her, which would mean a lot of explaining to a lot of strangers in order to get herself out of this mess.

He went to his desk and rifled through some papers. He seemed to find what he was looking for because he grabbed a few of them and headed for the door. "Ye may join me on deck."

"I'll be there in a minute." She had to find a way to make herself look more presentable first.

He hesitated for a moment in the doorway, his eyes meeting hers before looking away and leaving her.

"Get it together, Danielle. You're safe and you'll be reunited with Susanna in a little while." She chose to believe that scenario over the alternative. Her friend would never believe what she'd been through and was probably sure that she'd drowned. She got up and checked her clothes. They were still too damp to wear. "This dress is going to have to do."

She ran her fingers through her hair, and, finding an oval mirror hanging above a pitcher and bowl, she checked to see how she looked. After carefully braiding her hair, she turned her head from side to side. *Passable,* she thought.

Making her way out onto the deck the bright sunlight momentarily blinded her. Shielding her eyes with her hand, she noticed the men were all busy getting the ship ready to dock, so she did her best to stay out of their way. The sight of the island brought tears to her eyes. She hadn't thought she'd ever see land again and yet here she was gazing at Bermuda. The final destination on her trip. The sun was shining and a warm breeze wafted across the deck. She inhaled the freshness of the salt air and smiled to herself. This was going to be a story she'd be able to tell her grandchildren about one day.

CHAPTER 3

$\mathscr{B}$ermuda was nothing like she'd expected it to be. For one thing, the docks were crowded with other ships that looked a lot like *The Dagger*. There were no trucks or vehicles of any kind. She wondered if they weren't allowed on the docks here, although that seemed odd.

Jameson Mackall stood by her side as they disembarked to stand on the wharf. "Shall we find yer ship?"

"I can do it. I'm sure you've got lots to do. Thank you so much for everything." She glanced left and right, trying to decide which way to head.

"The docks are no' a place for a woman." He obviously thought that just because she was a woman, she needed a man to help her.

"I can take care of myself," she assured him.

A scowl spread across his face as his eyebrows once again collided. Danielle thought it was cute and smiled, pointing to them. "You're going to break those if you don't stop."

The expression on his face went from confused to serious in a flash, which made her laugh. It was too bad that this was goodbye. She wouldn't mind getting to know him better and seeing if she could break through that stern exterior. "I should get going. My friend is probably devastated about what happened."

"Ye should be careful, lass. This isn't New York, ye ken."

"Thank you for your concern, but I'll be fine." Should she hug him? He didn't look like the kind of guy who would appreciate that, but she thought she'd ask anyway. "Would you mind if I hugged you?"

The look on his face said no, but still he nodded his head in agreement. She approached, arms wide open and his body stiffened awkwardly. It seemed he didn't know what to do with his hands as she wrapped her arms around him. Pulling back, she rubbed his arms before letting him go and noticing the softness of the velvet fabric. "Nice jacket."

He didn't say anything. Instead he squinted his eyes as if trying to figure her out.

"Bye. Thanking you for saving me hardly seems enough, but it's all I've got."

He nodded as she turned to walk away. Looking back, she saw he hadn't moved from the spot where she'd left him. He was watching her as he stroked his chin and wearing a puzzled look that did not detract from his handsomeness in any way.

The farther she got from the ship, the more her shoulders tensed. Something wasn't right. The docks teemed with men who looked exactly like those on board *The Dagger*. Dirty, sweaty pirate types loaded and unloaded every ship she passed. The ships themselves all seemed to be sailing vessels. There wasn't a modern ship among them.

Danielle stopped and looked for anything that might tell her where Pier 17 might be. She hoped she had headed off in the right direction, although when she'd mentioned the pier number to Jameson he'd looked at her as if she had two heads. "I'll just keep walking." She was talking to herself, which was something she did when she was trying to figure out a puzzle of any kind.

A large rough-looking man bumped into her. "Pardon, Miss."

Someone squeezed her bottom from behind her, causing Danielle to jump. She spun around and was greeted by laughter. She turned again to walk away and ran directly into the man who'd just apologized for bumping into her. He, too, found the situation amusing.

Her throat tightened and her heart raced. Fear made her push her way through these rough looking men and coming across the first respectable looking person she'd seen, she asked, "Can you tell me where Pier 17 might be?"

The man looked up from some papers he'd been examining. "There be no Pier 17."

"Are you sure? I'm looking for a ship called *Neptune's Gold*. Do you know it?" She clenched and unclenched her hands as a sudden shakiness in her limbs left her feeling weak and out of control.

"I'm afraid not, miss." He went back to looking at his papers.

This wasn't good. How could she possibly have lost her friend, her ship and all of the people she was responsible for? A sick feeling settled in the pit of her stomach. Something definitely wasn't right.

Danielle decided to ask the question she wasn't sure she wanted to know the answer to. "I know this sounds odd, but can you tell me what year it is?"

Again he stopped what he was doing and looked at her. She saw pity in his eyes. "Miss, 'tis a strange question ye ask, but I'll answer ye. 'Tis the year 1724. We're in Bermuda in case ye're wondering about that as well."

"Thank you." She began to shake uncontrollably. The man reached out a hand to steady her, but she brushed it aside. She had to get out of here, but how? She turned away and began to run. She ran as fast as she could while wearing a dress that seemed determined to trip her up every few steps. Danielle headed back the way she'd come, passing the men who'd laughed at her and who now stared after her as she rushed by them.

Running blind was a term she'd heard used before and now she knew exactly what it meant. She ran and ran until she was out of breath and could go no farther. Hands on her knees and breathing heavily, Danielle looked up to see Jameson Mackall pushing through the crowd that had begun to gather around her. She stood, almost falling, but Jameson caught her.

His hands held her fast, stopping her fight or flight instincts and her irrational need to run as though that act alone would save her.

"What's wrong, lass? Has someone hurt ye?" He gazed over the top of her head seeming to search for a culprit. "Show me who and he'll regret the day he was born." His voice roared above the noise of the docks, obviously meant to frighten those around them. It worked because the men of the docks began retreating back to the work they'd been doing before she became the object of their fascination.

"No one's hurt me." She barely squeaked out the words, still so out of breath that it was difficult to speak.

"Then why do ye run like a frightened deer?" He drew back, still hanging onto her and tipping his head to the side to see her face better.

The kindness and concern in his eyes were unmistakable. Yes, he was a pirate. A real pirate, but her intuition was telling her she could trust him. "I don't belong here."

"Did ye no' find yer ship?" His voice was calm and the sound of it soothed her.

This was hard enough for her to believe. How could she possibly expect him to understand? "No." She watched as his eyes searched her face.

Jameson released her from his grasp. "Please doona run."

"I won't." She was touched by the softness of his voice. He wanted to help her and she needed his help more than he knew.

Jameson took her hand and placed it in the crook of his elbow. He covered it with his free hand. They walked through the throngs of men who had only moments before scared her, but now she was embraced in the safety Jameson afforded her as those same men hurried out of their path.

Now that she took the time to really look around, she saw what she should have seen all along. This wasn't the Bermuda she should have arrived in with *Neptune's Gold*. This was Bermuda of old. It was the Bermuda of three hundred years ago and it terrified her. "Where are we going?" It was impossible to keep her voice from shaking.

"A place more comfortable. Ye look as though ye're in need of a drink." He walked quickly, but took care that she could keep up.

"It's a little early for that, don't you think?" She wasn't much of a drinker and never before five o'clock. It was barely noon.

"I doona."

They turned onto a side road that led away from the docks. The difference was immediate in both sight and sound. Colorful houses dotted the street and well-dressed couples strolled arm in arm smiling and nodding to those they passed.

Beautiful matching bay horses pulled an ornate carriage that passed them by and stopped in front of a soft blue two-story building up ahead.

Jameson patted her hand. "Lady Charlotte. Just in time."

They hurried toward the carriage, arriving as a striking older woman was helped out by the footman who had rushed down the steps to greet her.

Looking up, the woman spotted them. "Jameson Mackall!" Her serious expression turned to joyous in the blink of an eye. "What a wonderful surprise. And who have we here?" She turned toward Danielle.

"Miss Danielle York, visiting from New York. This is Lady Charlotte," Jameson said.

The woman tipped her head and smiled warmly. "My dear, you've come a long way. Are you visiting family?"

"No, I..." They had no idea how far she'd actually come, but she couldn't find the words to tell them.

"She had a mishap at sea," Jameson explained for her.

Lady Charlotte's eyebrows shot up. "And you rescued her, of course."

"I just happened to be in the right place at the right time."

"How fortuitous." She directed her attention to Danielle. "He's a good man. Don't let his profession fool you." She dismissed her footman with a wave of her hand. "Please, come inside. I'll have Louisa prepare a little something for us."

Danielle glanced down at the beautiful dress Jameson had loaned her and saw that the hem was in tatters and the dress itself was ripped from all the times she'd stepped on it as she ran. "I've ruined the dress you let me borrow."

"'Tis only a dress," he assured her.

"Abigail's?" Lady Charlotte asked.

"Aye," Jameson confirmed.

She rolled her eyes. "She'll never miss it."

"No. She will no'."

Danielle wondered who this Abigail was and why she'd left her dress on board *The Dagger*. Thinking about something other than time travel and the unbelievable situation she found herself in was a distraction she needed in this moment. She'd think about the hard stuff later.

Jameson had always enjoyed his visits with Lady Charlotte Abernethy. He didn't see her nearly as often as he should, but she understood the life of a pirate. His mother's brother had lived in London and married Lady Charlotte. They were nobility there. Years ago they had left the comforts of London for the adventure of island living in Bermuda. Jameson's uncle passed away a few short years after their arrival and Lady Charlotte found herself alone. She could have returned to London, but she'd made a place for herself in Bermuda and had no wish to leave. She was a respected member of society and had a busy social life. Having no children of her own, she'd often told Jameson she thought of him as the son she'd never had.

Glancing Danielle's way, he knew something was terribly wrong. He'd seen the fear in her eyes and the way she looked at everything as though it were the first time she was seeing it. Even here in Lady Charlotte's drawing room, her eyes darted around the room as she examined the furnishings, ceilings and the lamps. The only thing he could surmise was that her time in the water had somehow addled her brain. He hoped for her sake that it was temporary.

"Danielle, I don't know you at all, but it seems you aren't feeling well. You look a bit pale." Lady Charlotte rang a small bell located on the fireplace mantle. "Perhaps some tea would help."

"I think we could both use a good tot of whisky," Jameson said. "Tea would be of no use in calming Danielle's nerves."

"Tea would be lovely," Danielle said, her voice still a bit shaky.

"We could put the whisky in the tea." Lady Charlotte laughed.

A servant Jameson knew well entered the room and waited for his orders. "Good day to ye, John."

"Good day, sir."

"John, please bring us some tea and whisky." Lady Charlotte glanced Danielle's way. "And something sweet. I'm sure Louisa has something in the kitchen."

John bowed his head in acknowledgment. "Of course."

Lady Charlotte turned her attention back to Danielle. "After tea, we'll find you a new dress to wear. That one has seen better days."

"Thank you," Danielle said. "It's very kind of you, but not necessary."

"You simply cannot wear that ragged dress around town. What will people think? If you will be staying here in my home, I will not have people believing I would allow you to dress that way."

"Be careful," Jameson teased. "She may wish to adopt ye."

Danielle looked as though she might argue with them, but before she could, John returned with a tray containing a floral teapot, cups, a crystal decanter of whisky and some small cakes.

"I'll pour, John." Lady Charlotte motioned for him to place the tray on the tea table in front of her.

John did as instructed and left them.

Lady Charlotte poured a cup for each of them and then added a splash of whisky, some cream and sugar. Handing a cup to Danielle, she giggled and winked.

Danielle seemed a bit apprehensive, but took a sip.

"Well, what do we think?" Lady Charlotte asked her.

"Better than I thought it would be." She took another sip, looking as if she were enjoying it.

"Your accent is unusual. Does everyone in New York speak this way?" Lady Charlotte sipped her tea and placed one of the small cakes beside her cup.

Jameson watched as Danielle looked his way before speaking.

"Not everyone." She helped herself to a cake and took a small bite.

"My, things have changed in the colonies, haven't they?" There was what appeared to be an amused tone to Lady Charlotte's voice.

"More than you know," Danielle answered.

Jameson wondered at Danielle's cryptic reply. What did she mean? The last time he was in New York, and it hadn't been that long ago, he hadn't heard anyone speaking with the accent Danielle had. His concern for her was growing. He wondered if he'd be able to help her.

"Jameson, would you show Danielle upstairs to my dressing room? I will speak with Louisa about our meal and then join you."

"I'd be happy to." He held out a hand to Danielle. She took it and he helped her up and then guided her up the stairs.

"You really don't have to do this," she said.

"Ye might as well give in. Lady Charlotte will insist. Once she's made up her mind, there's no changing it. It will make her happy to help ye."

"If it will make her happy, I guess I'll go along with it." Her reluctance was obvious. The reason for it was not.

"That is so kind of ye." He tried to control the sarcasm in his voice, but to no avail.

"Don't get me wrong. I appreciate it, but I'm not staying. I've got to find a way back home."

"To New York?" he asked.

"Yes, to New York."

"I can take ye to Charleston and ye should be able to book passage north from there."

"You'd do that for me?" She seemed surprised once again at his readiness to help her.

"Aye. I've business to attend to there. Nothing urgent, but something I should have taken care of long ago."

"When can we go?" she asked.

"In a day or two. The men need some time ashore and I'd like to visit with Lady Charlotte."

"You'll stay here, then." Lady Charlotte appeared in the doorway.

"Aye. We will," Jameson assured her.

"Good. I'll enjoy your company for however long I have it." She smiled at Danielle. "Now, if you'll excuse us, sir. We've a dress to find."

"I'll leave ye then."

Lady Charlotte followed him to the door and shooed him out before closing it in his face.

L aughing as she turned back to Danielle, she looked her over from head to toe. "I've got just the dress. The color will favor your hair and eyes."

"I can't thank you enough." Danielle glanced around at a room that looked very much like Lady Charlotte in its femininity.

"If you make my Jameson happy, it's the least I can do to show my appreciation." She picked up a brush from a nearby dresser and handed it to Danielle.

Danielle took it from her, feeling a bit embarrassed at how disheveled she must look. It occurred to her that Lady Charlotte thought she and Jameson were together. "Oh, Lady Charlotte, we're not a couple."

"Please, call me Charlotte. There's no need for formality here. You may not be a couple yet." Lady Charlotte undid the braid in Danielle's hair. "But I think you'll do very nicely."

"For what?" The brush she'd been handed hadn't yet been put to use. This whole conversation had her head spinning.

"To wed. He needs a wife and I'd like him to settle down. Give up piracy. I worry about him, you know." Charlotte took the brush from Danielle's hand and began slowly running it through her hair.

"I can imagine, but I'm not staying. I'm going back to New York." Danielle wanted to make that point very clear. Some way, somehow, she would get home.

"My dear, you may go back to New York, but you're not going home."

"What do you mean?" That was an odd statement coming from someone she'd just met.

"I mean that it is no longer your home."

Danielle was having a hard time following her. Did she know about the time travel, or was she just saying that because she wanted Danielle to marry Jameson?

Charlotte opened an armoire and started pulling out dresses. She set them aside as she continued her search. "Ah, here it is!" She held the dress at arms length. "Yes, this is the one."

A pale blue silk dress was held out for Danielle's inspection. The bodice was framed with embroidered flowers and cream-colored ribbons. Bell-shaped sleeves ended with a flourish of white lace. The skirt of the dress was bordered at the bottom third by matching embroidery and ribbons. "This is amazing!" Danielle had never seen a dress made with such attention to detail. It must have taken hours, if not days to create.

"Yes. I have a dressmaker in town who is very talented. Perhaps we'll take you to see her."

"You've been so kind. I couldn't possibly. I've no way to repay you."

"I can see that you aren't comfortable with my charity, but shall we say that when you wed Jameson you will be family and this is my gift for you." A warm smile appeared as she gazed at Danielle.

I'm not going to win this argument. Lady Charlotte had no idea that once *The Dagger* sailed, she would never see her again. She didn't wish to throw cold water on her dreams. It was obvious she loved Jameson and wanted the best for him. Danielle wasn't going to be able to help her in her endeavors. How could she? She didn't even belong in this time. All she wanted was to go back home. She didn't know how, but she would get there. She simply had to.

CHAPTER 4

Jameson waited for Danielle at the foot of the stairs. The expression of appreciation on his face was hard to miss.

"Ye look lovely," he said.

She smiled down at him before slowly and painstakingly making her way down step-by-step. The size of the skirt made it very difficult for her to see where she was placing her feet and she wobbled, sure that at any moment she would go tumbling downward and land at Jameson's feet.

Lady Charlotte had not only seen to her dress, but had her lady's maid style Danielle's hair in an updo with long curls draped over her shoulder on one side. She felt as though she were going to an elaborate costume party.

Thankfully, as she got closer to the bottom, Jameson offered her his hand. Once she was on solid ground in front of him, his hand wandered to the curls lying over her shoulder, brushing across her bare skin in the process. She held her breath until he moved his hand away. Something about his touch was both unexpected and intimate in a way she couldn't explain. She'd been touched many times by men, but it had never felt so familiar.

"Ye were gone a long while," he noted, still gazing at her with what appeared to be appreciation.

Maybe she was imagining things. She hardly knew him and he hadn't shown any interest prior to this. "It took some time to transform me from looking like a drowned rat into what you see here." She indicated the hair and dress as she waved her arms from head to toe.

A deep, soft chuckle that was barely audible to anyone but her caused her belly to do a flip-flop. "Ye were pleasing to the eye even as a drowned rat, but this is much better."

Danielle felt ridiculous. She wasn't a frilly girl. Hair down and with a slight curl was how she normally wore it. Slim and slightly curvy, her clothing style was typically classic, fitted and flattering to her figure. She liked heels for work and flats for weekends. How women of this time did it was beyond her, but she was certainly finding out.

"I thought ye might enjoy a tour of the town, Danielle."

The way he insisted on using her formal name and the way he said it, gave her goosebumps. No one called her Danielle. Her parents had when they were alive, but no one had since. He made her name sound almost seductive and she liked it.

"Okay. I'd like that."

He had that look on his face again, but this time instead of colliding eyebrows he had one cocked and Danielle found it irresistible.

"What is okay? I've no' heard that word before."

"Did I say okay? I don't know where that came from. I was trying to say all right." That didn't sound at all believable. She was going to have to be careful of her choice of words or she was going to have to tell him she was a time traveler. That would come at some point, but for now being a woman of the eighteenth century seemed to be working for her.

"Ye amuse me, Danielle." He held out his arm for her.

Danielle placed her hand where she'd come to know it was expected. He tucked her arm into his side, drawing her into closer contact. The heat of his body penetrated through the sleeve of her dress, up her arm and down to her core. Butterfly wings fluttered in her belly as she wondered just what might happen between them given time.

"Jameson, take good care of our guest," Lady Charlotte called down from the top of the stairs. "We'll sup on your return."

"Of course," he said, turning back and winking at her.

"Don't give her a hard time," Danielle whispered. "She seems to think you're going to marry me."

Jameson seemed to choke on his words. "Did she say that?"

They were headed down the steps to the street. "She did." Danielle was enjoying his discomfort perhaps more than she should, but she couldn't help it.

"Ye'll have to excuse her. She thinks every woman in town should marry me," he explained.

"It's the whole pirate thing. She wants you to stop." She glanced up at him and was once again taken by how handsome he was.

"I ken it."

They walked along, passing houses that although different in color, resembled Lady Charlotte's. At the end of the row of homes, they came to another street that seemed to contain shops and an inn. Danielle was intrigued. If she had to be in this time, it would be best to enjoy it. To look at it as an adventure she could use in her business if she ever got back to it. Silently reprimanding herself, she changed her thought to when she got back, not if. She'd worked hard to build the business with Susanna and she wasn't planning on giving that up.

The first shop they came to had a window displaying fabrics, dresses, and other finery. Danielle stopped to look, fascinated by the display.

"Would ye care to go in?" Jameson asked.

"Could I? I won't be a minute." She let go of his arm and was about to turn away.

"I'll go in with ye." He placed his hand on the small of her back and guided her toward the door of the shop.

"Really?" She was surprised he was interested.

"Why would I no'?" he asked.

She shrugged one shoulder and smiled at this man who seemed to be full of surprises.

As Danielle scanned the dresses, Jameson busied himself speaking with the shopkeeper. Out of the corner of her eye she noticed that he seemed to be shopping. She thought he must be purchasing things for Lady Charlotte. No wonder the woman loved him so much. He was very thoughtful.

After spending a good amount of time looking over the dresses, she joined him. "I'm good," she said.

"Aye. Ye are good," he replied, a puzzled look on his face.

She'd done it again. This time she didn't bother to correct herself. Did it really matter if he thought her odd? As soon as it was possible, she would be going back to her own time, although it disturbed her that she had no idea if it was even a possibility.

As they exited the shop, he handed her a package. "For ye."

"Me?" She pointed a finger at herself.

"Aye, is that so surprising?"

She held the mystery package in her hands, gazing down at it. "I don't know. What is it?"

"Ye can open it now, or ye can wait until we return to Lady Charlotte's."

She was never good at waiting to open gifts. "I'll open it now." Inside the package, she found a pretty pale blue purse that matched her dress, a brush, a comb and a small mirror, the handles of which were all encased in silver etched with elaborate depictions of flowers and birds. She looked up at him and watched a slow, sweet smile appear. "Thank you, but why…"

"Ye seem to have lost everything. I thought those items might be things ye'd miss the most. If there's anything else ye need, please allow me to obtain them for ye." Jameson took the package from her and led her down the street.

Danielle was so touched by his kindness that she missed half of the shops they passed. All she could think about was the man at her side and what he'd just done for her. The men she'd dated over the years had never been very thoughtful. Maybe that said something more about her choices than it said about the men themselves. She wished there was a man like Jameson waiting for her back in her own time.

"So what do ye think of St. George's?" Jameson once again placed his hand over hers and Danielle couldn't help but think that they looked like all the other couples she saw strolling past them.

"I like it. It's very different than I'd imagined it would be."

"In what way?" he asked, seeming truly interested.

What could she say? She couldn't tell him that it was missing the cruise ships, big resorts and streets filled with tourists. "It's just that it's nothing like New York." She knew that at some point she might have to share her secret with him, but not today. "Were all those ships we saw on the docks pirate vessels?"

He laughed at this. "No. Many were merchant ships come to port with goods needed by those who live here."

"It's such a beautiful place. I can understand why people would want to live here, but what is there for them to do for work?"

"Bermuda is known for its ship builders. Lady Charlotte owns several acres inland where they grow cedar trees. The wood is harvested for the ships that are built here."

At the end of the street, approaching the beach, they came upon a small wooden stand where a man called to them. A pile of coconuts sat beside him and as they approached, he cracked one open for them. Jameson paid the man with a coin from his pocket and then led her to a bench overlooking the beach.

"This is a coconut," he announced.

She didn't have the heart to tell him that she was well aware of what it was. He seemed thrilled to be sharing it with her.

"I'm sure ye've never had anything like it."

"How unusual," Danielle said, taking a sip as he offered it to her. She wanted to say, this would be great with some rum, pineapple and a tiny umbrella for decoration, but knew she shouldn't. "Delicious."

"Do ye truly think so?" Jameson asked.

"Yes. I do."

He offered her another sip and held it for her as she drank. "Thank you."

Jameson looked out over the beach to the ocean. "I could easily call this place home."

"Why don't you?" she asked. "It would make Lady Charlotte happy."

"Someday perhaps. For now I have a job to do."

She'd never thought of being a pirate as a job. "What do you mean?"

"I'm searching for a treasure that's been lost for years now. Buried somewhere by Christopher Plumb before he was caught and hung by the British. In the meantime, I'm searching for a Spanish galleon laden with gold."

"Inca treasure?" she asked.

He pulled away, eyeing her. "Inca treasure? Why do ye say that?"

"When the Spanish conquistadors arrived in South America, they pillaged gold from the Inca to bring back to Spain."

Jameson was silent and she realized she'd said too much.

"Ye surprise me, Danielle. Ye've much knowledge."

"The gold they took either made it back to Spain or is at the bottom of the ocean." Danielle was sure she was off with her timing. She'd done some research before booking the pirate cruise. Fascinated by the lore of buried treasure and sunken ships, she'd gone a little overboard in her reading. And now she wasn't sure she had her timing right. If she kept talking, she was going to dig herself into a deeper hole than she was already in. "Could I tell you something?" she asked, turning to Jameson.

"Of course. Anything."

"You might find this hard to believe. I'm having a hard time believing it." She bit her lower lip.

Jameson took her chin in his hand and brushed his thumb across her lips, stopping her from drawing blood.

She could stare into his eyes all day. They were dark pools beckoning her closer. Before she could get too drawn in, Danielle hopped up and looked away from him.

"Ye're no' planning to run again, are ye?" he asked.

"No." She turned back, wringing her hands and frantically

thinking this was all too much and Jameson would never believe her. He'd probably have her locked up somewhere for her own good.

"What is it ye wish to tell me?" His voice was soft and reassuring.

"Promise me that you won't think I've lost my mind." She was pretty sure he was going to.

"Why would I think that?" He took her hand in his and waited for her to speak.

"I'm sure you've noticed that I seem out of place here." It was a good start. She'd see where it led her.

"Aye, but ye've had quite the ordeal. 'Tis to be expected."

"You have no idea." Her stomach roiled and she felt as though she might be sick, but she had to tell him. He was the only one she *could* tell.

Jameson gazed up at her, waiting. He coaxed her back down where she sat facing him. "Come now. It can no' be so bad."

"It's worse than you could imagine."

He sat quietly waiting for her. He didn't push or prod her to tell him. This was definitely her decision.

"You remember I told you about the green sky and you said you'd seen it, too."

"Aye."

"Well, something strange happened to me. You see, I was on a cruise from New York with my friend, Susanna. We were taking a group of people on a corporate retreat." This wasn't going to get any easier to say if she dragged it on and on. "That cruise ship left New York Harbor in the year 2021."

Dead silence followed her announcement.

"You're not saying anything." She looked into his face, trying to read him, but his stoic expression gave nothing away.

"So ye're from the future."

It wasn't a question. Did that mean that he believed her?

"I am."

His eyes were focused on the horizon as he rubbed a hand across his jaw. "Do ye believe the green light had something to do with it?"

"Yes. The green light and the loud boom that rocked the ship. You don't seem shocked or surprised."

His gaze shifted back to her. "Nay. About two hundred years ago, an ancestor was rumored to have come from the future. She traveled back in time with the help of an emerald gemstone."

"Really?" She couldn't believe what she was hearing. She wasn't the only one this had happened to.

"Aye. I've heard the tale many times."

"And you didn't doubt it."

"Nay."

"So, if you believe that story, then you believe me?" *Please believe me.*

He sat tapping his lips with his index finger as he stared out to the surf. "I believe 'tis possible."

"Oh, thank you. I've been wanting to tell you, but I was so afraid."

"Ye need no' fear me, lass. 'Tis others ye need be wary of." He turned to face her. "Yer secret is safe with me."

"Should we tell Lady Charlotte?"

"That is yer decision, but I believe she would listen and no' judge ye."

It was a relief to have someone to share in her experience. Jameson believed her. She felt all the tension leave her body. The heaviness was gone from her shoulders and she felt lighter and more at ease.

"We should get back. Lady Charlotte will be waiting for us."

"**Y**our uncle told me the story many times. Your many times great-grandfather, Nick Mackall, had also traveled through time, so he was not surprised when Katriona told him she was from the future." Lady Charlotte was seated on a beautifully brocaded chair in the sitting room.

Jameson sat attentively at Danielle's side. His presence gave her confidence that with his help she could handle anything that came her way.

"Did she ever go back?" Danielle asked.

"No. I don't believe so. She had the emerald and was told she could use it any time she wished, but never did as far as I know. Had you heard anything, Jameson?"

"I seem to recall my father telling me that she did no', but there was someone, and I can't remember who, that traveled to the future and back again."

"I hadn't heard that," Charlotte replied.

"Maybe I need something like that to get back home." Excitement welled in Danielle at the thought that there were others who'd gone before her and that there was hope she could go home.

"Perhaps you need to wait for the green light to appear again. You say the moon was full that night?" Charlotte's full attention appeared to be on Danielle's problem.

"Yes. Do you really think I have to wait until the moon is full again?" Danielle thought that if it was the case, she would have to spend a whole month in this time. She wondered if she could do it.

"I don't know, my dear. I'm not an expert on this topic." She averted her gaze, which Danielle thought odd.

"If only I could find someone who was." If there were someone in charge of this time travel thing, she hoped they'd heard her.

"I believe that things present themselves to us when it is the appropriate time." Again she avoided looking at Danielle. This time she focused on her hands in her lap.

"I guess I have no choice in the matter. I'll just have to wait and see what happens."

"In the meantime, you can enjoy yourself here with me. Jameson will be leaving tomorrow for Charleston."

"I thought I was going with you." Danielle turned to Jameson. "I wanted to go so that I could find my way back to New York. From there, I might be able to go back to my own time."

"I was expecting ye to join me." Jameson assured her.

Danielle was relieved. She enjoyed Lady Charlotte's company, but her safety and security were found with Jameson. She couldn't possibly sit around here and wait for him to come back for her. "Lady

Charlotte, I hope you won't think me ungrateful. I've enjoyed my visit, but I can't stay."

"Please, call me Charlotte. No need for formalities. It has been wonderful having you with us, even for such a brief time, but I understand, my dear." She glanced from Danielle to Jameson with a mischievous grin.

"Shall we enjoy the delicious meal Louisa has prepared for us?" She stood and Jameson offered her his arm, escorting her into the dining room.

Danielle followed at his side.

The large wooden table was shined to a glossy finish and set with beautifully matched plates and silverware. Serving platters were laid out on the table. The meal consisted of a delicious fish stew.

"Freshly caught this morning," John said as he ladled some into Lady Charlotte's bowl.

Wine was poured for each of them and then John left them to enjoy their meal.

"This is wonderful," Danielle said.

"Louisa is the very best cook. She came with us all the way from London and has been with me ever since. She'll be pleased to hear you are enjoying the meal."

John returned to light the candles set around the room. "The sun is setting, Lady Charlotte."

The light outside of the windows lining the dining room walls was slowly fading.

"Thank you, John. We wouldn't want to eat in the dark."

He lit the last candle and left the room.

Jameson eyed Danielle across the table. She was a fascinating woman who'd found herself here in his time. Spending the day with her had been a pleasant adventure for both of them. No woman to this point had been as appealing to him as Danielle was turning out to be. His last dalliance had ended as quickly as it had begun and Jameson had vowed not to allow himself to believe he was in love ever again. What he'd shared with Abigail was not love, it turned out, but it took him a long while and many months at sea to understand that.

It would certainly be interesting learning more about Danielle. He'd already noted several things about her that were in stark contrast to the women of his own time. She seemed very independent, freely said what was on her mind and she didn't put on airs. She was herself and that was the best compliment he could give anyone. Danielle might be just what he needed. There was no chance of a long-term relationship since she'd only be staying long enough to find her way back to her own time. It would also put Lady Charlotte's ideas about marriage to rest for the time being. He'd marry someday, but for now his ship and his crew were his main concern. Of course finding treasure, whether aboard a Spanish galleon or buried beneath the sand on one of the many islands dotting the Caribbean, was always on his mind.

CHAPTER 5

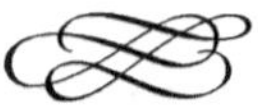

The sun was barely up, but the docks were bustling and the men of *The Dagger* were ready and waiting for their captain to board.

"Good day to ye," Hawes said, as he helped Danielle aboard. If he thought it odd she was with his captain, he didn't let it show.

"Good day." Danielle greeted him with a warm smile.

"Are ye coming with us to Charleston?" he asked, looking from her to Jameson.

"Aye, Hawes. She will be joining us. Is everyone aboard?" He glanced around at his men before turning back to Hawes.

Hawes also took note of the men on deck. "Aye, Cap'n."

"Set sail when ye see fit," Jameson ordered.

"We were only waiting on ye, sir. Everything is ready." Hawes signaled to the men. A moment later, they were hard at work. They pulled up the gangplank as a man on the docks tossed the rope that had been holding *The Dagger* secure up to Hawes who easily caught it and then waved to the man.

Jameson placed a hand at her back as they walked the length of the deck. "We can stay on deck, if ye wish."

"I'd like that." She leaned on the nearby rail and gazed back at the docks, which were now slowly receding. "I'm sorry you had to cut your visit with Lady Charlotte short. I know you'd wanted to spend some time with her."

"I'll be back before she knows it. 'tis important that we get ye home."

"How long will it take to get to Charleston?"

"Three days if all goes to plan." Rather than watching his men, he seemed happy to let Hawes handle them and more interested in focusing on her.

Danielle enjoyed the attention. "Why wouldn't it?" she wondered.

"It depends on what we might come across on our journey."

That didn't sound good. "What do you mean, come across?"

He smiled, seeming to sense her unease. "Possibly the galleon we seek, or a storm. One never knows what is just beyond the horizon."

Danielle didn't like either one of those possibilities. She'd been hoping for smooth sailing and no nausea. "If you see the galleon, what are you going to do?"

"Well, the men would no' be happy if we passed it by." He stood close by her side, blocking her from the view of the crew.

She imagined it wasn't very ladylike to be leaning the way she was and tucked her bottom back under her as she straightened up so that her hands rested on the rail. "Right."

"No need for worry, lass. I'll protect ye and keep ye from harm."

"Yes, but can you save me from seasickness?" She slid her eyes to the side to look at him.

"I believe I can aide ye if needed," he said in all seriousness.

She'd been joking, sure that he didn't have some magic pill that would aid her and surprised when he said he could help. She believed him and not just because she had to, but because he'd shown her in so many ways over the past few days that despite the pirate label, he was a gentleman and a man of his word. "I'd like to go to your cabin."

"Hawes, please escort the lady to my cabin."

Hawes came running at the sound of his name. "Aye, Cap'n. Come along, miss." He took hold of her arm.

"Hawes, the lady can walk on her own." Jameson shook his head and chuckled.

"Sorry, sir."

She was disappointed that Jameson wasn't escorting her, but realized he was the ship's captain and he had work to do. She hoped to see him later. Danielle felt terrible that he would be giving up his cabin to her once again and wondered what the sleeping arrangements were like below deck.

Wandering the cabin in search of something to alleviate the boredom, Danielle came across a deck of cards and sat down behind Jameson's desk to play solitaire. Laying them out, she appreciated the way the kings, queens and jacks covered the entire card wearing crowns and flowing robes in red, black, gold and white. These would be valuable antiques in her time and yet here they were a simple deck of cards and nothing more. Thankful to have found them, it would make up for her lack of phone, computer or Susanna to occupy her. Still, it would be a long three days.

A knock at the door surprised her. "Yes."

The door opened and Hawes entered carrying a tea set. "Cap'n says ye may need some of my ginger tea."

"Thank you. Did he say why?" she asked.

"So ye will no' feel sick when the ship rolls."

"That was very thoughtful of him."

Hawes set it down on the desk. "I see ye found the cards."

"Yes. I hope it's o… all right that I use them."

"Cap'n won't mind."

"How long have you known Jameson?"

"Only the past three years. Before that I sailed with his uncle, Rourke Mackall. He be the governor of Manta Cay now." He was quiet for a moment before continuing, seeming unsure whether he should. "When Cap'n Rourke gave me his ship to captain, it was no' what I wanted, but I could no' turn him down. I would no' disappoint him. I captained *The Dagger* for a whole year." He shook his head as he spoke. "I'm grateful Jameson came along when he did."

"I understand. You like working behind the scenes."

"I'm sorry." He held a hand to his ear, as though he couldn't hear her.

"You prefer helping the captain rather than being the captain."

"Aye. That be true." He turned to leave, but before he did, he turned back to her. "The captain be a good man. Treat him well." He seemed a bit embarrassed at this point. "Drink yer tea."

"I will." To prove the point, she picked up the cup and took a sip.

He nodded and left her.

Hawes hadn't been at ease as he'd spoken to her, but he'd made his point. It seemed everyone wanted her to know what a good man Jameson was. They also were quite the bunch of matchmakers. "I'll bet he has no idea what they're all up to." She had to laugh at the thought.

As she dealt out another round of solitaire, Danielle thought about the strange turn her life had taken. Out of nowhere, she found herself in a different time where she couldn't imagine she'd ever fit in. Yet she had. She was capable of handling anything being thrown at her. These people were real and not a figment of her imagination. They had hopes and dreams, fears and joys. These men were pirates, but that didn't mean that she couldn't communicate with them. It was something she was good at. She'd done it with her business. Tapping into her clients' needs had been what made her successful.

Her thoughts were interrupted by a commotion on deck. Sounds of men shouting and running came through the door of the cabin loud and clear. She hopped to her feet, unsure of what to do.

The door flew open and Jameson rushed in accompanied by two other men she had seen but hadn't yet met. Brushing past her, he went to his desk and unfurled a nautical chart. "We're here." He pointed to a spot on the chart. "The galleon wasn't anywhere to be found a few days ago."

"Then who is she?" the taller man asked. He was neatly dressed, shaved and all in all not someone she'd expect to see on *The Dagger*.

"It could be a Spanish warship, but whoever it is, they are bearing down on us. We must outmaneuver them." Jameson was all business and Danielle had to admit it was a very attractive quality.

Hawes rushed in, out of breath. "Sir, they look to be heavily armed. They've begun firing on us."

"Return fire. Have the men ready. We can outrun her, but we've no' a moment to waste."

"What's going on?" Danielle asked. A loud thud sounded above them, causing her to jump.

"Nothing for ye to worry about," Jameson said.

"It sounds like *you're* worried."

He took a deep breath as he straightened. "Aye. 'Tis for me to worry. No' ye."

"Mackall, can you not see she's frightened. 'Tis her first time aboard a pirate ship." The man seemed anything but bothered by what was happening around them.

Jameson gazed at the man and then at her. "I'm sorry. We are being stalked by a Spanish man-o'-war. If we can no' outrun them, we'll have to engage in close battle."

Danielle was determined to hide her fear. She hid her hands and their shakiness from view in the folds of her dress. "Is there anything I can do to help?"

"Nay. Stay below deck for the time being. Sutherland here will stay with ye." He pointed to the man who'd just spoken.

"I'll happily take care of the lass." Sutherland looked her up and down before smiling at Jameson.

"Sutherland…" Jameson growled.

The man chuckled at this. "Ye should introduce us, should ye not?"

"Danielle York, this is Edward Sutherland," he said through gritted teeth.

"A friend of many years. 'Tis a pleasure." Edward gave a slight bow in her direction.

Jameson opened the cabin door and yelled out, "Lynk, get the ship ready to run."

"Aye, Cap'n," came the reply from on deck.

"I promised I would let no harm come to ye. I intend to keep that promise." Jameson exchanged a threatening look with Edward before leaving them.

"Do not think him a coward." Edward kept his eyes focused on the desk top.

"I don't. He has the lives of everyone aboard to be concerned with."

"He does. 'Tis a large task, but one he was made for. There's no finer man to be found." He looked up at her and smiled.

"You're overselling him a bit, aren't you?"

He laughed as he rolled the map up and placed it back with all the others behind the desk. "I like you. You'll be good for him."

"Why is everyone trying to make us a couple? We've only just met." There seemed to be no let up on the number of people who were matchmakers in this century.

"Is there something wrong with wanting a friend to be happy again?"

"Why? Is he sad?" The thought made her think again about the man she'd been getting to know. He always seemed in control of every situation, including this one.

Sutherland shook his head and made a face that if it hadn't been for the predicament they found themselves in would have caused Danielle to laugh. "That woman. I cannot remember her name. Lady something or other. She took his heart when she knew she should not."

"And what about him. Did he let her?" It would be hard to imagine that Jameson played no part in whatever had happened with *that* woman.

"He did." Again the charming smile appeared.

"Let me be clear. I'm not staying around. It wouldn't be fair to either of us to start something we couldn't finish."

"Could your mind be changed?" One arched eyebrow and a slight smirk appeared.

"I don't think so." How could it? She had a business to run first and foremost. Besides she'd miss her friend, her phone, basic electricity and hot showers. There was no way she could live in this time.

"Ah, think. Interesting choice of words. You don't *think* so." He thumped his fingers across the desk.

"You remind me of my friend, Susanna." She could imagine having this exact conversation with her friend. The only difference being that Susanna didn't have an English accent. She was always on Danielle to find a man.

"Does Susanna have a man?" he asked, sounding intrigued.

"No. She doesn't. Do you have a woman?" Two could play this game.

A loud, hardy laugh burst from him. "I must admit I do not."

"Then maybe you should concentrate on finding someone for yourself before you try your hand at matchmaking." There. That should put an end to this conversation.

"Abigail was not good for him."

"Abigail." That's the name Lady Charlotte had mentioned. "I think I borrowed her dress. Hopefully she won't want it back. It's hardly the same dress now that I've made a mess of it."

"She should have taken it with her when she left, but I believe she left it here as a reminder. You did him a favor by taking it away."

"Where is she now?" Danielle asked, her curiosity piqued.

"Charleston."

"Isn't that where we're going?"

"It is. She was to be married, so she is no longer a threat."

"Hopefully he won't run into her." A surprising need to protect Jameson welled up inside of her. The woman had obviously broken his heart from what she'd been able to put together and it would probably be painful for him to see her again.

"Yes. What are your plans once we get there?"

"To find my way back to New York."

"New York! You're a long way from home."

"So I'm told."

"What brought you to Bermuda?"

"*The Dagger.*" She liked being sarcastic and Edward seemed like the perfect man to be sarcastic with. "Sorry. I couldn't help myself. I was on my way to Bermuda with friends."

"And they dumped you in the ocean. Not such good friends." It was his turn to be sarcastic.

"No. I fell overboard and no one saw me," she lied.

"Surely they're searching for you." Edward straightened the cuffs of his shirt as he spoke.

"It's been days. They've probably given up." Sadly, that was probably very true.

"Come." He led her to the windows. It was clear that *The Dagger* was moving at a good clip. "Do ye see it?"

A large ship was some distance behind them and it appeared they were not gaining ground. "We're outrunning them."

Edward tapped his finger on her arm to make his point. "Aye. Jameson has seen to it."

A volley of cannon fire sounded from the Spanish warship, causing Danielle to jump once again. Her relief had been short lived.

"Doona worry. They are too far to hit us." He sounded like this was commonplace, something he was very used to.

"Why would they try then?" The reality of being aboard this ship was hitting her over the head. Danger could appear at any moment. She'd thought pirate ships were part of a romantic adventure until now. She'd done her research for the cruise, but had carefully ignored the darker details of pirate life.

"'Tis a warning. The Spanish galleon we seek is nearby." He turned away from the windows.

The distance between the two ships grew and the cannon fire stopped. She let out the breath she'd been holding.

"There, ye see. We're safe once again." He threw his hands up in the air matching his *I told you so* attitude.

Danielle had to admit he'd done a masterful job of taking her mind off of the peril they were in. Edward opened a drawer in the desk and removed a decanter and two small glasses.

"One for each of us," he said. "To soothe what's left of your nerves and celebrate our escape."

He poured two and handed her one. "I don't really want this." She wrinkled her nose at him.

Downing his own shot, he took hers and did the same. "If you no longer have need of me, I'll see if Jameson does."

"What exactly do you do other than act as a very good distraction?"

He chuckled at her question, but his answer was short and sweet. "Quartermaster."

She had no idea what that was, but before she could ask him, he was gone. Now alone in the cabin Danielle had time to contemplate the strange situation she found herself in. She wanted to go home, but at the same time was finding herself more and more attracted to Jameson. If she fell for him, would she be able to leave him behind? It was a question she wouldn't have anticipated a few short days ago.

CHAPTER 6

"We did more damage than we received," Jameson explained. "I'll see the shipwright in Charleston for repairs."

"Will we make it there?" Danielle asked, biting her lower lip.

"Ye're determined to damage those pretty lips of yers," Jameson noted. "'Tis a small leak, nothing that can no' be plugged and nothing that will sink us."

That was a relief. The last thing she wanted was to end up floating in the Atlantic Ocean again. "So you think I've got pretty lips?" She had to admit it gave her a bit of a thrill every time he glanced her way with more interest than she'd seen from any man in a very long time. The fact that it was Jameson Mackall made it all the more enticing and enjoyable. She was now doing her best to tease her way into a conversation about anything other than this ship.

He stopped what he was doing and took her chin in his hands. Taking a long slow look at her lips, Jameson turned the tables on Danielle. Her belly did a little flip-flop as she wondered if he'd kiss her.

"Aye. Verra pretty." He let her chin go and turned back to his desk leaving her deflated and wishing he was still talking to her about her lips.

"So when will we arrive in Charleston?" If he was done checking out her lips, she might as well know if their travel plans were still on schedule.

"If all goes well, tomorrow." He straightened some papers on his desk before looking up at her.

"What does that mean?" she asked, remembering their close encounter with the Spanish warship.

"Doona worry yer lovely self, lass. We'll be there tomorrow." He brushed past her and out the door, lightly tracing her jaw with his finger as he did so.

Again, more compliments. He was definitely flirting with her and she liked it. A warm, tingly sensation made its way through her body causing her to smile. They'd made a connection on the island, but they'd hardly had time to explore it before they were back aboard *The Dagger* and headed to Charleston.

The anticipation of what might happen between them ran through her head. Tired of the inside of the cabin and hoping to do more flirting with the handsome captain, she ventured out after him, but wasn't fast enough. He was already across the deck and busy speaking with Hawes and Lynk. At least she could walk the deck and hopefully not get in the way.

Edward joined her as she walked, but was immediately reprimanded by Jameson. "Sutherland, leave the lass be."

"All right, Mackall." He turned to her. "If ye'll excuse me. I believe I've made the man jealous." He blew her a kiss as he walked towards his captain.

Danielle rolled her eyes at him and laughed. As she continued on her walk, she noticed Jameson's stern gaze on her. It seemed Edward was right: Captain Mackall appeared quite perturbed by what he'd just witnessed. She ducked her head and looked out to the ocean, hiding her smile. If she had to be stuck on a ship in the eighteenth century, she was happy it was this one and even happier to be enjoying her time with Jameson.

"How are ye feeling, Miss?" Hawes asked as she passed him.

The daily dose of ginger tea had really helped. She'd been skeptical at first, but if she found herself feeling at all nauseous, Hawes would see to it that she had a cup. "I'm fine, Hawes. Your ginger tea is a miracle. Thanks to you, the seasickness is practically gone."

Danielle wouldn't have believed it possible to embarrass a pirate, but Hawes turned quite red. "Happy to be of service. Ye ken the longer ye spend asea the better. What I mean to say is ye grow accustomed to it." He continued walking beside her and when she looked his way in question, he said, "The captain asked me to walk with ye. Sutherland, ye ken."

Laughter bubbled from Danielle's lips. "He needn't worry about Edward."

"Pardon me saying, Miss, but the man hasn't seen a pretty lass he hasn't wished to…to…"

Hawes was really quite sweet and Danielle couldn't help but feel sorry for him as he tried to explain Edward Sutherland to her. "Don't worry, Hawes. You can assure Captain Jameson that I'm quite capable of taking care of myself and of making my own decisions when it comes to men."

"Aye, miss. I'll walk with ye just the same."

They walked up and down the deck several times before Danielle decided she'd had enough and headed back to the cabin.

"I'll bring yer meal soon," Hawes called to her as she walked up the stairs to the captain's quarters.

"That's very sweet of you." She didn't have to look back to know he was blushing or to know that Jameson Mackall was still watching her every move.

The *Dagger* weighed anchor out in the harbor. Jameson instructed the men to find the shipwright and have him repair the ship. He then took a skiff with Edward and Danielle into Charleston. He would be relieved to get Sutherland away from her. Once they set foot on solid ground, he knew his friend well enough to know he'd be seeking out one of the many women he visited when in port and he'd lose interest in Danielle. Not that it mattered to him, but he didn't wish her heart to be broken.

As much as he hated to admit it to himself, his attraction to Danielle had grown since they'd first fished her out of the water. She was unlike any woman he'd known before and she was standing at his side waiting for him. "Shall we?" he asked.

"Where are we going?" She placed her hand in his arm and looked up at him with a gaze that seared itself into his heart. He was going to have a hard time letting her go.

"To the inn. I'll get ye a room and ye can rest."

"I'd love to see Charleston." Her voice was filled with an eagerness that was endearing.

"No rest?" He thought sure she would need it after three days on the ocean as well as a near miss with a Spanish warship.

"No. I've been resting on the ship for the past three days. I like to be busy."

"If yer wish is to see Charleston, then that is what we shall do."

She smiled up at him with those perfect lips she liked to bite. He'd stopped her each time, but more for his own comfort than hers.

Jameson reserved two rooms at the inn, which was the finest in all of Charleston. From the furnishings to the food, it was a feast for the eyes and the belly. Danielle seemed fascinated by it all, which brought him great satisfaction.

"Dinner will be served at one if ye wish, Captain Mackall." The innkeeper was a tall and very thin man who knew Jameson well from his many visits to the city.

"We'll return at that time." Jameson led Danielle back out onto the street in front of the inn. He remembered their walk in Bermuda and how much he'd enjoyed her company.

"I'm excited to explore colonial Charleston," she said as they began to walk.

"Do you ken the history of the city?" he asked.

"I do."

"Ye could tell me its future." Jameson couldn't imagine it would be much different, but then he had no idea what the future would be like.

"I could. I could tell you a lot of things."

"Can ye tell me where I can find Christopher Plumb's treasure?"

"No. I don't know anything about that. I did do a lot of research on shipwrecks from this time period and there were a lot of them. There's a lot of gold at the bottom of the ocean."

"Unable to be retrieved then."

"Not in this time, but in the future, there are people who have the equipment they need to find it."

"They must be verra rich."

She shrugged a shoulder as if it didn't matter to her. He wondered if a trip to the future would give him what he sought.

"Ye'll tell me all ye know at a later time then?" His curiosity about the future had gotten the better of him. He'd never been one to seek the advice of soothsayers, but this was different.

"Of course."

She smiled that sweet smile he was coming to believe was just for him, but he wondered about Edward and what he'd seen going on with them. "What of Edward?"

"I'm sorry?" she seemed confused by his question.

He hadn't meant it to come out, but there it was. "Edward Sutherland. Ye have feelings for him?"

"Absolutely not!"

Good. She seemed insulted by the implication. "He is interested though."

She laughed at this. "He's just trying to make you jealous."

"Is he now?" Not surprising, he thought.

"Yes. I thought you were friends." Danielle's eyes sparkled with the humor she seemed to find in his relationship with Edward.

"We are. We've a long history of vying for the affections of the same lass."

"I wouldn't waste my time vying for mine."

He was taken aback by her assertion. "Are ye no' worthy of our attentions?"

"I wouldn't say that. It's very flattering, but I don't know what the future holds for me."

"What if ye can no' return to yer own time? What will ye do?" He glanced down at her wondering at her bravery in the face of what must certainly be a jarring turn of events.

"I haven't really thought about it. I like to be optimistic that I'll find my way back home."

"I promised I'd help ye and I will if 'tis what ye wish." He hoped it wasn't what she wished. He wanted her to stay. It was becoming more clear to him with each passing day.

"You're a good man, Jameson. I can understand why your friends want to protect you."

"Protect me from what?"

"I don't know. Maybe from yourself."

What on earth did she mean?

"There's a woman headed our way who's waving at you."

Jameson had been so focused on Danielle that he failed to notice.

"Jameson!" Lady Abigail Matheson called.

She was the last person he wanted to see. He gripped Danielle's hand on his arm.

"Are you all right?" she asked, placing her free hand on his arm.

"Jameson! What a surprise!" Lady Abigail was right in front of them now. There was no avoiding this meeting.

"Abigail. I wasn't expecting to see ye here." His back stiffened and his hold on Danielle tightened.

"Charleston is not as vast a city as London. How have you been?" She stared up at him with an adoring gaze he remembered from their time together on the voyage from London.

He glanced down at Danielle who had moved in closer to him.

"And who is this?" Abigail eyed Danielle with what looked to be a painted-on smile.

"This is Lady Danielle York, my fiancée." He hoped Danielle would accept her new title. If not, he would be quite embarrassed.

"I'm pleased to meet you. Jameson, I had no idea." Abigail cocked an eyebrow as she gazed at Danielle before looking back at him with an odd expression for a married woman.

"We are quite in love. Are we no'?" He silently pleaded with Danielle and luckily, she was willing to go along with this farce.

"Very." She gazed adoringly up at him and for a moment he thought that perhaps she really did love him. "It's a pleasure to meet you, Lady Abigail."

"Jameson and I are old friends." Abigail's nose pointed upwards. "Perhaps he's told you about me."

"He's never mentioned you. I wonder why?" Danielle looked to Jameson, playing her part to the hilt, and expecting an explanation.

"My dearest, it was of no importance." He smiled his gratitude to her for going along with him.

Lady Abigail seemed irritated by this slight.

"Jameson is taking me shopping. He is so generous." Again Danielle looked up at him with the same adoring eyes.

He would buy her whatever she wished if she kept up this pretense.

"Aren't you just the dearest," Lady Abigail said, her voice dripping with sarcasm.

"Apparently I am. We must go." Danielle tugged on Jameson's arm and began to walk away.

"Perhaps I'll see you this evening. A gala is being held in Governor Nathaniel Johnson's honor." Lady Abigail tugged on his sleeve, stopping him in his tracks.

"We've no' been invited." Jameson turned away, joining Danielle as she walked and hoping that would be the end of it. He had no wish to spend more time with Abigail.

"'Tis not necessary." She called after them. "All are invited. I'll send my carriage for you. Are you at the inn?" She waited for his reply, not moving from the spot where they'd left her.

He wasn't going to be able to get out of this. No excuse came readily to mind. "Aye."

"We'll speak more then, Miss York. I want to learn all about you." She hurried on her way.

Danielle gazed at him and then using one of those unusual sayings of hers, said, "She's really something."

"Something, aye."

"What was your relationship with her? As your fiancée, I believe I have a right to know." She was teasing him now.

"Ye are a clever lass." Clever and beautiful, he thought. "'Tis a long tale."

"I've got nothing but time." She patted his arm with her free hand.

"Her husband, Lord Matheson, passed away over a year ago and she was in need of immediate passage to the Carolinas. Because the Mathesons were friends of Lady Charlotte, I was asked to see that she arrived here safely. She was to marry her husband's brother."

"So women actually did that? I mean, do that. I'd read about it, but I couldn't imagine it was a real thing."

"The man offered and she accepted," Jameson explained.

"So it wasn't forced on her?"

"Nay. It was her choice to marry him. I was told it was a convenience for them both. Her husband left her penniless and his brother, who was a wealthy man, needed a wife."

"And how did you fit into this?"

This was an uncomfortable conversation for him. One he had been hoping to avoid, but Danielle was persistent. "I told ye. I was tasked with bringing her here."

"That can't be all there is," she said, elbowing him in the side.

Jameson got the distinct feeling that she was enjoying his discomfort. "My *friends* talk too much. We had a… How can I put this?" He didn't wish to have this conversation with her, but she'd asked and he felt that since she'd agreed to the pretense of being his fiancée, he had no choice. "Shall we say we enjoyed each other's company while she was aboard *The Dagger*."

She wasn't saying anything. Had he offended her? "I'm sorry. Ye must be shocked."

"Not at all. She's a grown woman and you're a grown man. Things happen."

"It does no' trouble ye?"

"Times are different where I'm from. You had a brief affair. I don't know if it ended badly, but based on the fact that you made me your designated fiancée, I'm guessing it did. Do you still love her?"

"I never said I loved her."

"You didn't have to. I've heard it in so many ways since I've known you. Lady Charlotte, Hawes, Edward...you."

He let out an exasperated sigh. "I did think I was in love, but came to realize it was nothing more than an infatuation. 'Tis done." He was through talking about it. The only thing he wanted now was to enjoy the company of the woman at his side. The woman who challenged him and seemed capable of making him doing anything she wished him to do.

Danielle couldn't believe this juicy bit of colonial gossip she'd just heard. She felt Jameson's pain. He'd obviously been in love, or lust, and had been hurt when it ended. She knew what that felt like. She rubbed his arm. "I'm sorry."

"No reason to be sorry. As I've said, 'tis done."

"Are we going to the gala?" she asked.

"Would ye like to?"

"How often am I in the eighteenth century? I would love to."

Jameson chuckled and Danielle was happy he wasn't mulling over his meeting with Abigail. "Ye'll need a proper dress."

"This one won't do?" she asked, glancing down at the dress she'd been given by Lady Charlotte.

"Come, we'll get ye something pretty and verra much yer own."

She could easily see herself falling in love with Jameson. He was so thoughtful and kind. "You really don't have to."

"I wish to."

"I usually buy my own clothes."

"Ye've no money."

He had her there. She had nothing but what she'd been given. It was an unusual feeling for her. She was independent and resourceful in her own time, but here she was relying on the kindness and generosity of a man she was coming to find was perhaps everything she'd ever wanted.

They found a dressmaker on Broad Street. A dress was chosen. Danielle let Jameson pick since he knew better than she what would be appropriate for the gala. He had very good taste.

"Blue is yer color," he said. "It makes yer eyes shine."

The dress was the deepest shade of blue, with ecru lace at the neckline and draping from the bottom of the bell-shaped sleeves. He also purchased some of the things she'd need to wear beneath it and a shift for sleeping.

Danielle didn't have the heart to tell him it was a waste of his money. She'd only be using them for a short time, but she'd already decided she would take them with her to remember him and this unbelievable adventure she was on.

She'd thanked him numerous times since she met him. Words of thanks hardly seemed enough for all he'd done for her. Danielle counted herself lucky he'd been there to save her and that he'd then taken her under his wing and continued to feel responsible for her. A sudden rush of warmth overcame her as they stood outside the door to her room at the inn. She kissed his cheek.

His arm snaked around her waist, holding her close to his chest. "What was that for?" he asked, his voice a low rumble in her ear.

"Can't a lady kiss her friend?" She was in trouble now. Sexy man trouble. The best kind of trouble. She could feel it all the way down to her toes.

"Only if the same goes for her friend." He dipped his head, gently kissing her lips, before slowly and deeply kissing her again.

If Danielle had been tingling before, she was now on fire. Heat surged through her and left her aching in all the important places. She hoped he would kiss her again, but instead he let her go.

"Ye should rest before this evening's gala." He opened the door to her room.

"I might need help getting ready." Danielle eyed him through fluttering lashes.

He winked at her. "I'll have the innkeeper send someone up."

She walked into the room and turned to invite him in, but he closed the door before she had a chance to speak. It had been a long time since a kiss had thrown her that off kilter and it took her a minute before her heart slowed down and her breathing went back to normal. She wanted more of that – more of him. Danielle was torn between her need to return to her own time and the very real feelings she was developing for Jameson. She had no idea how this was all going to end, but for now she was going to live in the moment.

CHAPTER 7

"I'm so happy you could attend." Lady Abigail greeted them as soon as they walked in. She'd seen them arrive from across the room and made a beeline straight for them. Danielle thought she looked beautiful in her rose-colored gown, her dark hair worn in the style of the day and expensive looking jewels hanging round her throat.

The gala was being held in a private home just outside of the city. Danielle was impressed by the elaborate decorations. Candles lit the rooms, which were decorated in neutral shades of ecru and tan. The furnishings were exquisite. Chairs and settees were upholstered in soft blue damask and the tables and chair legs were beautifully carved wood.

Lady Abigail was intent on Jameson, taking hold of his free arm and guiding him inside. Apparently, Danielle was along for the ride as she held onto Jameson and followed at his side. They were introduced to Lord Camden, the man hosting the evening's event, and then eventually to the governor.

"Governor Johnson, I'd like to introduce you to Jameson Mackall and..." It was obvious Lady Abigail had conveniently forgotten Danielle's name.

"Lady Danielle York," Jameson supplied.

"It's a pleasure to meet you both," the governor said, seeming truly pleased, despite the many people waiting to see and speak with him.

"They're visiting Charleston. I'm hoping to convince Jameson to stay." Abigail held tightly to Jameson's arm as she spoke. It was as if she were afraid he'd run away if she let go.

Danielle couldn't believe the nerve of this woman. She'd dumped Jameson and now she was cozying up to him. Where was her husband?

"Where is your husband, Lady Abigail?" Danielle asked, as they were whisked away from the governor and toward a table of food and drink.

"I'm widowed. My husband was killed in a hunting accident not so very long ago." She stated this in a very matter-of-fact way and with little emotion.

Danielle glanced Jameson's way to see a surprised expression on his face. "I'm so sorry."

"I had no idea, Abigail. My condolences." He seemed uncomfortable. His whole body tensed as he looked past them and seemed to be scanning the crowd.

"I'm doing well. He left me with a lovely home and enough money to live comfortably for the rest of my life." She smiled a sweet, pretty smile his way.

Strange that she would immediately speak of being well off after the death of her husband. Danielle couldn't imagine marrying a man she didn't love, but it was obvious that it was exactly what Abigail had done.

"I wonder if I might borrow Jameson for a moment or two. I wish to speak with him privately." She sent that same sweet smile Danielle's way.

Jameson looked as if he were about to object, but Danielle didn't give him a chance. "Of course. I'll be fine," she assured him.

"Ye doona mind?" he asked, appearing worried.

"No. Go. I'm sure you have a lot to catch up on." Inside she was feeling all sorts of feelings she didn't think possible. Worry over losing him. Surprised to feel that way. Last but not least, raging jealousy.

He's not yours, Danielle. He never was. Danielle wandered around the room, nodding politely to those she passed. The experience she'd wished to have by attending this gala had taken a turn and now she felt out of place and uncomfortable without Jameson by her side. It was something she wasn't used to. Back in her own time she was always in control and could talk to anyone about anything. Being alone in a room full of strangers had never been a problem, but now it seemed daunting. After taking a few more turns around the room and not seeing Jameson or Abigail, she made her way through the room and out to the front drive. Flustered and out of her element, she realized she had to find a way back home. *I don't belong here.* It was very clear to her now. Playacting the part of a woman from this time period simply wasn't going to work for her.

"Ye seem distressed, my dear." An older gentleman who didn't seem to fit in here anymore than she did surprised her by appearing silently at her side. She stared at him, startled into silence. "Domnhaill MacCreary at yer service."

"Danielle York," she replied, introducing herself.

"What troubles ye? Perhaps I can help." He seemed sympathetic to her plight.

"I'm trying to find my way home." She failed to mention that home was three hundred years in the future.

"And where would that be?" he asked, sounding truly interested.

"New York."

"Ah, a fine city indeed."

"Yes, it is. And one I must get back to." Danielle glanced around at the carriages sitting idly. The drivers all stood in a group chatting with each other. She had no idea which was the one she'd arrived in.

"I may be able to assist ye. I'm headed there meself." He had a warm smile and friendly demeanor.

"You are?" She took a good look at the man. He was old enough to be her father and while he was rough around the edges, she wasn't getting any vibes that he was dangerous in any way.

"Are ye here with anyone?" He glanced around as if searching for someone.

"I was. I mean I'm with Jameson Mackall."

"Jameson. A good friend. We've known each other for years." He peeked over her shoulder one more time. "Where is he? I haven't seen him in some time. Shall we go find him?"

"He's with Lady Abigail Matheson. She wanted to speak with him privately. They went somewhere, but I haven't seen him since."

Domnhaill laughed. "One can always count on Jameson to be surrounded by beautiful women.

"Can they?" She hadn't known him very long. Maybe she was only seeing what she wanted to see and ignoring the fact that he was an unmarried pirate. She supposed it was completely possible that he had a woman in every port. Danielle peeked back at the house, hoping to see Jameson. She was disappointed when she didn't. The happy chatter of the guests was in complete contrast to how she was feeling. "How far is the walk back to the inn in Charleston?" As she asked the question she realized how ridiculous it was. She was in a place and time she was unfamiliar with. She couldn't possibly walk there on her own.

"Why walk when ye can ride with me? I'd be happy to escort ye to the inn. We'll discuss getting ye back to New York on the way."

"I'd truly appreciate it." She didn't want to wait around to find out that Jameson was getting back together with his ex and wouldn't be able to help her anymore.

Domnhaill signaled a carriage waiting nearby. Once it was in front of them, he helped her inside and joined her. He tapped on the roof with his cane and the carriage began to move. Domnhaill waved out the window to someone and laughed.

"I can't thank you enough," Danielle said.

"No need to thank me. I'm happy to be of assistance and in a way ye'll be helping me."

She couldn't really see his face in the darkness of the carriage, but his voice sounded jovial enough. "How so?"

"Jameson will be relieved to know ye're safe with me."

Danielle was feeling confused now. "I'm sorry. I don't understand how that helps you."

"Ye'll see, me dear. Ye'll see."

That was a strange response. Maybe this hadn't been the best idea. She'd allowed her jealousy and disappointment to cloud her judgment. She knew better than to take a ride from a stranger. Danielle would never have allowed this to happen in her own time. It seemed time travel had affected her good sense. There was no doubt it was best that she leave, but perhaps she should have waited for Jameson.

Jameson wasn't happy about leaving Danielle behind. He couldn't stop thinking about her. Seeing Abigail again hadn't had the sharp sting he'd expected only a few short days ago. He found that with Danielle by his side, Abigail's light had dimmed in his eyes.

"Jameson, I'm so sorry that I left you and never said goodbye. I want you to know that if I'd had a choice I would never have gone off to marry Lord Matheson."

"Ye had a choice and ye made it." It was a fact. One that no longer bothered him.

"You must understand. As a widow left without a penny it was important for me to secure my future. I've done that now." Abigail clutched his arm as she guided him out to the garden. "'Tis good for both you and I. You'll never have to go to sea again." She stopped walking, took his hands and gazed up at him. "I still love you, Jameson."

"I doona feel the same, Abigail. I'm sorry." It felt good to say those words to her.

"You can't possibly mean that. I know you have a fiancée." She continued to hold tight to his hands. "She'll never be able to give you what I can."

"Yer wealth is no' attractive to me. Danielle can give me so much more. She is the one I want. Now, if ye'll excuse me, I've left her long enough." He removed Abigail's hands from his own. He had to find Danielle. He had to tell her how he felt. His heart was lighter than it had been in years.

Entering the house from the back garden, he searched for Danielle. Crowded with guests, it was near to impossible to see where she might be. He wandered through the crowd, moving from one part of the room to another and then into the side rooms. She was nowhere to be found. He was about to check the front of the house when he heard his name being called.

"Jameson!" Edward Sutherland appeared in front of him, wearing an enormous grin. "Where's Danielle?"

"I was about to ask ye the same question." Jameson was worried. Where could she have gone?

Edward eyed him suspiciously. "You lost her. Did you do something to upset her?"

"'Tis possible." Guilt washed over him.

"I think I see what upset her and she's headed this way." Edward's eyes were focused behind Jameson.

He turned around to see Abigail rushing toward him. "Abigail, I doona have time for this now. I'm looking for Danielle."

"Did she leave you?" She wore a smug, self-satisfied little smile. "I'm not surprised. One of the other guests saw her speaking with a gentleman outside not long ago. She left with him in his carriage."

"Who was it?" He had to find her. She could have put herself in danger without even realizing it.

"They didn't say."

"I must find her, Sutherland." He rushed out the door with Edward right behind him. "Why would she accept a ride from someone she does no' know?"

"I'll get my carriage. You should ask around to see if anyone knows who she left with." Edward hurried away in the direction of a row of waiting carriages.

Asking everyone he saw, Jameson couldn't believe that no one knew the gentleman she left with. All he'd gotten was that it was an older man, unusually dressed for such an affair and that they'd spoken for a while before leaving.

The carriage drew to a stop and Edward flung the passenger door open for him. "Don't worry. We'll find her."

As the carriage traveled down Broad Street, Danielle was distressed on seeing that they had passed the inn without even slowing down. "Your driver missed the inn. He can stop here. I'll walk back." She did her best to control her voice, not wanting the man to know she was worried.

"Why return to the inn when me ship is docked in the harbor? We'll be on our way to New York in no time."

"But my things." She had to get back to the inn. Whatever this man wanted from her, she wasn't going to give him.

"I'll send someone back for them, or better yet, we'll buy ye new things. Would ye like that?" He chuckled and tapped her leg lightly with his cane. "It was good fortune that I met ye tonight, lass. I'm no' one who enjoys hobnobbing with people such as those at the gala, ye ken."

"Then why were you there?" She adjusted her dress and moved out of the reach of his cane.

"I was hoping to find someone like yerself. Someone who would be of service to me."

The prickly sensation on the back of her neck told her she was in trouble. She'd foolishly gone with Domnhaill when she would have been better off waiting for Jameson. The carriage stopped at the docks and Domnhaill got out, extending a hand for her to take.

"I'm not going with you." She stubbornly retreated to the far side of the carriage, folding her arms across her chest.

"Ye've no choice, me dear." He reached in, grabbing her by the wrist and pulling her from the carriage. She struggled with him, trying to break free, but he was stronger and larger than she was.

"Create a stir if ye must. No one will dare to help ye." He chuckled as she tried to free herself from his grasp.

She noticed men on the docks had stopped what they were doing and watched, but none of them moved toward them. "Help!" she yelled over and over again before being muscled into a skiff. A hand was placed over her mouth.

"Ye can stop now. They've all heard ye." Domnhaill spoke close to her ear, causing her to flinch.

The skiff set out at a breakneck pace. The men rowed it faster than she thought possible. Domnhaill held her tightly to his side. "You're hurting me!"

"I would no' want ye to fall overboard."

She wouldn't want that either, but it seemed preferable to what was happening to her at the moment. Squirm as she might, there was no way to escape his grasp.

As they approached the ship, a man at the front of the skiff called out orders to those on board. A rope ladder was thrown over the side and Danielle found herself being hoisted over another man's shoulder as he made his way up to the top and she was handed over to yet another man.

Domnhaill was right behind them. "Lock her in me cabin." The man who'd carried her up the ladder grabbed her arm.

"Let me go!" Panic welled up inside her. She did her best to calm down, despite the fact some man she didn't know had his hands on her.

"I'd go along quietly if I were ye," Domnhaill called after her.

She gave up. There was no point in struggling. She'd be better off saving her strength for when she had a plan to escape. Although the farther they got from shore, the less likely that was to happen. She'd been a fool to allow herself to be kidnapped. If she'd stayed and waited for Jameson, even if it was only to hear he was staying with Lady Abigail, she'd be safe. He'd promised to keep her safe and he had until she'd made it impossible for him to do so. Danielle wondered if he'd look for her or if he'd even notice she was missing.

J ameson and Edward arrived back at the inn. They immediately went to her room and found she hadn't returned. Jameson noted the things he'd given her were placed neatly on a dresser and Lady Charlotte's dress was laid across the bed where she'd taken it off.

"She's no' here." He paced back and forth across the room.

"Something just occurred to me. When I arrived tonight, I saw Domnhaill MacCreary leaving in a carriage. He waved to me."

"And ye're just telling me this now?" Jameson was angry. "That information would have been useful earlier."

"My apologies, but I saw no one with him," Edward replied, sounding contrite.

"We may be too late. What if he's leaving Charleston with her?" Jameson glanced around the room and before leaving he gathered the purse he'd given her, placing the comb, brush and mirror inside. When he found her, he wanted her to have them.

Jameson and Edward spent the rest of the night searching for Danielle. They asked everyone they came across if they'd seen her, but no one had.

"They're gone." He felt defeated.

"I'm sorry, my friend. 'Tis my fault." Edward sounded and appeared truly contrite.

"'Tis Domnhaill MacCreary who's at fault," Jameson uttered through gritted teeth. When he got his hands on that man, he'd regret ever taking Danielle.

Jameson went over the events of the evening. His first mistake was leaving her alone to speak with Abigail. He owed the woman nothing at all, but somehow felt he needed to hear her out. All the while he'd left Danielle alone and unprotected. He had unknowingly participated in her disappearance.

His fondness for Danielle had grown and the kiss they'd shared in the hall outside of her room had moved him both physically and emotionally. He had to find her. If anything happened to her, he'd never forgive himself.

"We should get some rest," Edward was saying. He placed a hand on Jameson's shoulder.

Shaking it off, Jameson said, "I can no'."

"Just a few hours. You need to sleep. You'll be awake and alert enough to continue soon enough."

Jameson hated to give up, but Edward was right. Fog was engulfing his brain. It would be wise to stop for now, but only for now. He would never give up. He would find her no matter how long it took.

They returned to the inn. Jameson went to Danielle's room and lay down atop her bed. If she came back, he wanted to be there. He gave Edward his room and instructions to awaken in two hours' time. They would eat something and return to their search. Nothing would stop him from finding the woman he'd come to love.

CHAPTER 8

Stomping around Domnhaill's cabin, Danielle's focus was on the one thing that seemed impossible - escape. If she couldn't escape, perhaps she could bargain with the man, but what did she have to offer him other than herself, and *that* simply wasn't an option.

The door opened and Domnhaill entered. He walked straight past her and to his desk where he sat in an oversized leather covered chair. "Well, Miss, what are we to do?"

"I don't have that answer. I thought you knew exactly what you were doing? What do you want with me?"

"Ye see, I'm searching for gold." He sounded as if he were speaking to one of his peers instead of to a woman he'd just kidnapped.

"Isn't everyone?" she asked, giving him a bit of sass.

The scowl he wore told her he wasn't amused by her comment.

"I don't have any if that's what you're thinking," she said.

"No, but I do need money to continue me search." He sat still for a few moments staring at her as if in a trance and making Danielle quite uncomfortable. A map on his desk caught his eye and he moved to roll it up and held it in his hand. "I imagine yer family in New York would pay anything to get ye back."

Stunned by this, Danielle moved to the desk. "Are you holding me for ransom?"

A soft chuckle escaped his lips. "Aye. I believe that would be exactly what I'm doing."

"I have no family in New York." She worried he wouldn't believe her and, if he didn't, how was she going to convince him?

"Where are they then?" He sat forward in his chair, staring intently at her.

"I have no family."

"Ye're an orphan?" He seemed incredulous.

"I'd never thought of it that way, but yes. My parents are both gone and I've no brothers or sisters, aunts or uncles."

He looked her over, moving from behind his desk to her side. She inched away, unsure of his intentions. Domnhaill's fingers touched the fabric of her dress. "Don't touch me."

"'Tis no' me intention, lass. How could ye afford such a fine dress if ye've no one to buy it for ye?" He was much too close for comfort now.

"Back in New York I have a job, I can buy my own clothes."

"What kind of a job?" he asked, seeming genuinely curious.

"I organize parties." It would be ridiculous to try to explain the whole time travel thing to him. Keeping it simple was best.

"Ah, ye're a strumpet!" He seemed delighted with himself for coming to this conclusion.

"I am not!" One thing she definitely didn't want to do was encourage that fairy tale.

"Then where'd ye get the dress?" he challenged.

"Jameson purchased it for me."

"Did he?" His eyes widened as he tipped his head, seeming pleased with this information.

"I just said he did."

"Hmmm...I bet he'd pay a nice sum to get ye back." He scratched his beard as he gazed towards the ceiling.

"I wouldn't know."

"Ye must be special to the man. Why would he spend money on ye?"

"Because I lost all of my belongings."

He didn't appear to be listening to her anymore. "There *is* something I want from him. Something I've coveted for some time."

"What is that?" she wondered.

"*The Dagger.*"

"His ship?"

"Aye. 'Tis a fine vessel."

"You already have a ship."

"I've more than one ship and *The Dagger* would be the finest of them all. A fleet of pirate ships would be difficult to defeat. Especially one led by *The Dagger.*"

Domnhaill held tightly to the rolled parchment in his hand and paced the floor with it. "Aye. The plan is a good one." Moving to a row of books beside the desk, he placed the map behind them, checking to see if Danielle was watching, which she was. "Doona touch it, do ye ken? I'll cut off yer wee fingers if ye dare."

"I won't, but why are you hiding it?"

"I trust no one. No' even the men aboard this ship. Once I have *The Dagger*, I mean to find me treasure."

Danielle's heart sank. She'd put herself in this position and now she was dependent on Jameson giving up his ship for her. How likely was that to happen now that Abigail was back in the picture?

When Jameson refused the exchange, what would become of her? What did pirates do with people who were no longer of any use to them? She shuddered at the thought.

Jameson quickly ate the food that the innkeeper had been placed in front of him. He wasn't hungry, but knew it would be important to sustain him through another day of searching.

Once again, they went throughout Charleston in search of Danielle. He was hopeful that Edward had been right when he said he saw no one with MacCreary in the carriage. The men at the docks had been no help. If they'd seen or heard anything, they were keeping it to themselves. He enlisted his crew to help. With so many men making their way through shops and taverns, as well as homes and farms on the outskirts of the city, he'd been confident they'd find her, but luck wasn't on his side. The sun had set and they still hadn't discovered her whereabouts.

"We should check the docks again," Jameson said. The last thing he wanted to do was leave Charleston without having done a thorough search.

"I was thinking the same," Edward replied.

They made their way to the wharf and other than the normal activity, everything seemed quiet. If they didn't find her tonight then it was probable that MacCreary had her. That created a whole new problem. He had no idea where the man had gone.

"'Tis a fool's errand. We'll no' find her tonight." He was about to turn away when a man emerged from a darkened corner and handed Jameson a piece of paper. "From Cap'n MacCreary," he said, before hurrying away.

"What does it say?" Edward asked.

"I can barely see it." He squinted his eyes and moved the paper closer to his face, but to no avail.

A man walked by with a lantern. "You there." Edward got his attention. "We need some light."

"Aye." The man obliged and stood nearby while Jameson read the note.

"Well" Edward asked.

"Domnhaill's got her. He is holding her for ransom." He crushed the paper in his hand.

"What does he want?"

Jameson dropped his hands to his side as the man retrieved his lantern and walked away.

"Well," Edward asked again, his impatience evident.

"*The Dagger*. He wants *The Dagger*." Jameson's voice was low and filled with rage.

"Your ship! You cannot allow it." Edward clenched his fists before taking the paper from Jameson and reading it.

"I've no choice. For now 'tis more important to save Danielle." He looked out toward the darkness that engulfed both sea and sky. His only thought was for her.

"I never believed I'd see the day when a woman was more important to you than your ship." Edward placed a supportive hand on his shoulder.

"Nor did I."

"We'll need to round up the men. They'll be at the tavern." Edward slapped him on the back and started walking.

Jameson joined him. "We must hurry. The note says they're headed to Spanish Point. We're to meet him there in four days' time." Thoughts of Danielle at the mercy of MacCreary and his crew tore at him. She had come to be the most important person in his life in such a short time. He wasn't about to let any harm come to her. If he had to relinquish his ship, he would do it.

our days was a long time to wait for someone, but Danielle hoped in her heart that Jameson would come for her. It didn't seem likely. He'd reconnected with the woman he'd loved and lost and it appeared she wanted him back.

Domnhaill's ship was anchored off the coast of a place he'd called Spanish Point. She'd been allowed on deck where she leaned on the rail enjoying the warm tropical breeze gently caressing her face and hair.

"Are we near Bermuda?" she asked a passing crewman.

"Aye."

That was promising. When it was clear that Jameson wasn't going to come for her, she might be able escape the ship. They weren't too far from shore. She thought she'd be able to swim it. "Does anyone live on this island?"

The man looked in the same direction she'd been looking. "I doona see anyone." He then walked away and left her.

There were no other ships anywhere in sight. Even if she could get away, where would she go? If the island were deserted would she be able to survive? Danielle headed back to the cabin to await her fate, but before she could get there a shout came from above. There was a ship on the horizon.

Domnhaill appeared with spyglass in hand. Holding it to his eye, he smiled broadly. "'Tis *The Dagger*."

Danielle couldn't believe her ears. Jameson was coming for her. Her heart was filled with a joy she hadn't thought possible. Brushing away the happy tears now stinging her eyes, it was clear he still cared about her.

"Back to me cabin, lass. Ye're to remain there until I come for ye." He gave her a gentle shove in that direction.

Once there, Danielle paced back and forth. She couldn't believe Jameson was willing to give up his ship for her. How would she ever repay him? He'd surely resent the fact that he'd had to give up his ship. As she paced, her eyes fell on the books and she thought about the treasure map. She couldn't imagine Domnhaill would have continued to leave it there, especially since she'd seen him hide it. He seemed the suspicious type and so she was sure he would have found another hiding place for it. If she could find it, she'd give it to Jameson. It might not get his ship back, but if he could find the treasure he could use it to buy another. She lifted a book out of the way and was surprised it was still there. Quickly tucking it into the bodice of her gown, she replaced the book knowing that she'd just put herself in grave danger. If Domnhaill noticed it missing, he would know exactly who had it.

The *Dagger* moored alongside Domnhaill MacCreary's ship *The Savage Wolf.*

"I see ye've come for yer lass," Domnhaill shouted to Jameson.

"Aye. Where is she?" His eyes scanned the deck of the ship.

"Safe in me cabin." Domnhaill moved to the ship's rail, seeming quite pleased with himself.

"Did ye harm her?" Jameson was doing his best to keep himself from doing anything that would put Danielle in jeopardy.

MacCreary laughed. "Would I tell ye if I did?"

"Doona test me, MacCreary," he growled.

MacCreary brushed him off with a wave of his hand. "Meet me onshore. I'll bring the lass."

Jameson instructed his men that they were not to cede the ship unless they heard directly from him.

Taking Hawes, Lynk, and Edward with him, they boarded the skiff and headed for shore.

"Cap'n, are ye really planning to give yer ship away?" Hawes asked.

"Doona worry. If I do, we'll get it back in no time." He was focused on the task at hand. His worry was for Danielle. *The Dagger* would be back in his hands in short order, he had no doubt.

"Ye sound confident," Edward said.

"How?" Hawes wondered.

"I've a plan."

"Care to share it with the rest of us?" Edward asked.

"I will when I have a better idea of what he's up to."

They were greeted by MacCreary and his men. From the moment he'd left the ship until he set foot on shore, Jameson hadn't taken his eyes from Danielle. She stood between two of MacCreary's men appearing fearless and possibly happy to see him if he was to judge by the slight smile on her lips.

The men gathered in a circle above the tidal line. "Are ye ready to hand yer ship over to me?" MacCreary didn't seem able to keep the glee from his voice.

"Are ye ready to hand Danielle over to me?" Jameson glanced around at the men. They were all armed to the teeth. Any attempt to leave with Danielle *and* his ship would result in a battle both on shore and at sea. He didn't wish to risk her being harmed in the melee. His plan, it seemed, would have to wait.

"Doona get any ideas, Mackall. My men will no' hesitate to shoot the lass if need be."

"Ye may take the ship. I'll no' fight ye."

"Good. 'Tis better for all of us if ye doona."

Mackall signaled to his men on board *The Dagger*. They understood that when they received the signal from him, they were to surrender the ship. "The men will stay with ye. I've spoken with them about it. They'll give ye no trouble and I imagine ye'll be needing a crew."

"'Tis verra thoughtful of ye." Domnhaill beckoned to his men and they followed him to the skiff he'd brought ashore. "I believe we'll take yers as well."

The two men guarding Danielle left her and hopped aboard Jameson's skiff. She didn't move as she watched them row away from shore.

"What happened to the plan?" Edward asked.

"Poor timing. We'll get her back. I'll be damned if I let MacCreary have her."

He glanced back to where Danielle stood. "Excuse me, Edward." He walked back toward her, relieved she seemed no worse for wear. "Did he harm ye?"

"No." She shook her head and looked down at her feet.

He took her hand in his. "Why did ye go?" His voice was soft. He wasn't angry with her, but he didn't understand.

"Lady Abigail. You still love her, don't you?" she asked, still avoiding his gaze.

"No. If ye had waited for me, ye'd ken that."

She raised her eyes to meet his. "I'm sorry. I'm sorry for all of this. You're right. My feelings were hurt and all I could think about was going home."

"I'm flattered to ken yer feelings were hurt because ye thought I loved another, but ye worried needlessly."

"I know that now. What happened between you two?"

"She told me she loved me still. Abigail thought I'd be happy to know and was disappointed to find that my heart belonged to another."

"Oh, you mean the whole fake fiancée thing."

"No. I mean ye." She glanced away and taking her chin delicately in this hand, he turned her so she would see the sincerity of what he was saying. "Ye've captured my heart."

Swirling thoughts of love and excitement caused Danielle to feel a bit light-headed. She wanted to tell him that he had captured hers as well, but instead she stood their grinning and sucking in deep gulps of air. Maybe she hadn't heard him correctly. "Could you say that again."

Jameson chuckled as he pulled her into his chest and held her close enough to his heart that she could hear it thudding away. "I said that ye've captured my heart."

Flustered wasn't something Danielle ever was, but it seems she was experiencing all kinds of firsts lately. "Jameson, I... you mean even after I lost your ship? You're not angry with me?"

"How could I be angry with ye? It wasn't yer fault that MacCreary kidnapped ye."

"Well, it kind of was. I shouldn't have trusted him."

"Perhaps no', but my guess is trust him or no', the outcome would have been the same."

"I feel terrible about *The Dagger*. How are we going to get her back?" She wished she could stay tucked in his arms forever. She felt so safe and secure there.

Jameson's head rested softly atop her head. "All is no' lost. I'll get her back. 'Tis no' for ye to worry about."

There he was telling her not to worry again. She was good at hiding it, but if he knew anything about her, it should be that she worried all the time about everything. Her worry was a catalyst to solving problems, which she was very good at. But now, besides worrying about his ship, she was worried about how they were going to get off of this island.

Danielle gazed up at Jameson, appreciating the man he was and realizing how lucky she had been to be rescued by him.

"Are ye going to kiss me, lass? I've bared my soul to ye and ye just stare at me." A mischievous grin appeared on his lips.

Danielle reached up and pulled his head down to hers. Their lips met in a delicious kiss which repeated itself over and over again.

They reluctantly pulled away from each other to find Hawes, Lynk and Edward seated on the sand staring out at the departing ships. "What are we to do now?" Hawes asked.

"Get up off yer arses and follow me. We'll be walking to Tucker's Town." Jameson took hold of Danielle's hand and led her down the beach. The others followed along behind.

"Why are we doing this?" she asked.

"'Tis part of the plan." Jameson sounded a lot more confident than she felt.

"Oh, the plan ye've got to get *The Dagger* back." Edward smirked.

"Ye'll see. There's nothing here for us. At least in Tucker's Town we can get food and a place to sleep."

"Cap'n, is there a tavern? I'm in need of a drink," Hawes said.

"There is," Jameson assured him.

"How long is the walk?" Danielle asked.

"It could take from four to six hours' time."

Six hours of holding Jameson Mackall's hand suited her just fine. If it were just the two of them, it might even be romantic. Instead they were forced to listen to Edward complaining through most of their walk. They stopped and rested regularly. It was quite warm and the dress she was wearing was oppressive. A bathing suit would keep her cooler and more comfortable in this unrelenting heat.

Taking a peek back at the three men following along behind them, Danielle noted they were all sweating and wiping their brows. Hawes was the oldest of the bunch. It was hard to know how old any of them really were, but if she had to guess, Edward looked to be about thirty, Lynk maybe a little bit older and Hawes seemed to be in his fifties.

"How old are you?" Danielle tugged on Jameson's hand to get his attention. He was pretty focused on where they were headed.

"Five and thirty. Ye?"

"Thirty."

"And yer no' married?"

"No."

"Did no one want ye?" She could tell he was teasing by the cocked eyebrow and half smile.

"I'll have you know I'm a pretty hot commodity in my time."

"Yer words amuse me." He flashed a toothy grin.

She laughed. He really was enjoyable company. Still unsure of how this time travel thing worked, she wondered what would happen if she could go home. She was really connecting with Jameson on a romantic level and she'd hate to give that up, but could she really live here in this time? It was a question she'd been asking herself ever since her feelings for him had begun to develop. Of course, there was no guarantee that she'd ever be able to return home and if that were the case, she'd be happy to stay with Jameson. He was everything she'd ever wanted in a man. He was kind, caring, strong, protective, intelligent, and a true leader. In other words, he was pretty perfect.

CHAPTER 9

Tucker's Town was a small, sparsely populated place with one tavern that did double duty as an inn. There were a few houses built here and there around the town, which was named after a former governor of Bermuda, George Tucker. Danielle knew this because she'd done a considerable amount of research on the island before planning her ill-fated cruise. The town had an interesting history and she couldn't believe she was actually getting to see it back before luxury homes were built along the peninsula.

"Are we staying here?" Danielle asked, wondering if there were enough rooms upstairs in the tavern to house all of them.

Jameson held a chair out for her to sit before sitting beside her at a round wooden table that had seen better days. "Nay. When 'tis dark we'll head to the beach. One of the men from *The Dagger* will be meeting for us. In the morning, we'll head for St. George's."

"We're going to sleep on the beach?" she asked.

"'Tis a far sight better than this place."

Taking another look around at the dinginess of the tavern, Danielle had to agree.

They ordered a pitcher of Bibby, which Danielle found out was made with fermented palmetto berries. Cassava pie with chicken and an onion tart were also brought to the table. She wasn't sure what she had been expecting, but was pleasantly surprised. The food was delicious. They ate and drank, ordering two more pitchers of Bibby before Jameson paid their tab and they made their way to the beach.

Lynk and Hawes started a fire, which was more for light than heat, and everyone sat around it and waited. The men took turns watching for Jameson's man to arrive and when it was his turn, Danielle asked if she could join Jameson as he strolled up and down the beach.

"Aye. I'd be glad of the company." He took her hand again in that familiar way they'd established since her second rescue.

"Thank you for coming for me," she said. "You've rescued me twice now."

"I'd rescue ye as many times as needed." His voice, soft and low, reassured her.

Butterflies erupted in her belly, furiously flapping their wings as joyful satisfaction settled there, quickly followed by the uncertainty of her future here in this time.

Surrounded by darkness and far enough away from the prying eyes around the fire, Jameson reached for her.

Danielle went willingly into his arms and tipped her head up to meet his lips with her own. Her hands tangled in his dark locks as his settled on her hips. A flush of warmth engulfed her as she let her heart lead the way.

The moment would have become more heated, but the men they'd left behind hooted and whistled their approval and Danielle realized they could still be seen by them since the lantern Jameson had placed on the ground beside them illuminated them perfectly. She smiled up at Jameson. "No secrets here."

He laughed and wrapped an arm around her shoulders as they continued to walk. "I think no'."

Danielle was disappointed, but she knew that it was perhaps for the best that they take their time. The last thing she wanted to do was to break his heart. He meant so much to her. She would do anything to keep from hurting him.

A light appeared offshore as the waves lapped at their feet. "'Tis our man," Jameson said, lifting the lantern high.

They watched as the small boat got closer and closer until it ran up onto the beach. Jameson helped pull it farther on shore and greeted the lone man aboard.

"Owen!" He clapped the man on the back. "Did ye have any trouble?"

"No' a bit. MacCreary is headed to St. George's, so I did no' have far to row."

"Good. Get some rest. We'll set out in the morning."

Owen joined the others while Jameson turned to her. "I wish to walk more with ye."

"All right." They held hands and walked along the shoreline. The moon had been full on the night she'd fallen overboard and over the past several days had lost some of its fullness but still shined brightly enough for them to see where they were headed. It twinkled on the waves as they rushed to the shore. The smell of the salt air and the sound of the churning water made for a perfect pairing as they walked. Danielle rested her head on his arm, holding his hand with both of hers.

"Do ye still wish to go home?" Jameson asked, his voice tinged with concern.

"Right now, in this moment, no." She gazed up into his handsome and caring face. "I'm enjoying this time with you."

Danielle was doing her best to live in the moment and to let things play out as they would, but she knew that if there was a way to get home, she'd have to take it.

"I don't want to hurt you. I know you've been in love before and that when Abigail left you it broke your heart."

"Doona think me weak. I am no'. My heart was no' broken," he assured her.

"You can say that all you want, but I don't believe you." Everything she'd seen since she'd met him told Danielle that he was a man who cared deeply for those he was close with. It only seemed natural that

Abigail had taken his feelings and tossed them aside when she'd left him.

"Believe what ye like. I ken the truth of it."

They stopped and looked back down the beach. The fire was now a small dot in the darkness. Danielle thought about what he'd just said. Despite the fact that she didn't want to ever do anything hurt him, she couldn't deny the attraction between the two of them was more powerful than her willpower. "I think it's safe enough for you to kiss me again." She tipped her head as she gazed into his eyes. "If you want to, that is."

"Och, I want to."

A thrill ran through her body from head to toe. She couldn't remember kisses ever having so much power over her. There was something about this man that turned the heat up to scorching whenever his lips touched hers.

Jameson sat down on the sand and held out a hand to her, drawing Danielle down beside him. His kisses were soft and gentle at first, gaining more passion with each touch of their lips and then tongues. She wrapped her arms around his neck and pulled him down to lie beside her. Caressing his face with her hand, she drank in the look of him. His dark brown eyes, aquiline nose and strong jaw were perfect in her eyes. Her fingers ran over the scruffy stubble along his chin and then combed through his hair, which was soft and curled over the collar of his shirt. She was determined to burn the memory of him into her mind so that no matter what happened or where she ended up, she could call on that memory and he would be there with her on this beach. She would feel the closeness and the heat of his body as he removed any space between them. His hand at her back held her in exactly the position she wanted to be. He wanted her as much as she wanted him. The evidence rested hard against her thigh.

Jameson's breath tickled her ear as he kissed the sensitive spot beneath. A soft moan escaped her lips as another louder sound broke through, shattering the moment.

"Jameson!" Edward Sutherland called from only a few feet away.

"Edward!" Jameson's growl sounded both anguished and angry. "Ye could no' wait for us to return."

"I'm sorry." He was doing his best to look contrite, but the impish smile he wore seemed to say he was anything but sorry. "We've had an idea. A way to get *The Dagger* back."

Danielle wiggled out of Jameson's grasp and stood, straightening her dress as she did.

"Danielle," Edward nodded his head to her.

"Edward. Perfect timing." It seemed the universe was trying to keep them apart by throwing road blocks in their path at every turn. Again she thought it might be for the best.

"I apologize. It was not my intention to stop you from..." He waved his hand around in the air as if that would explain it.

Danielle liked Edward. He could be annoying, but she sensed that he meant well. It was just that the only thought in his head at any given moment seemed to be about himself.

"Well, what do ye want?" Jameson wasn't even trying to hide his irritation.

"We were speaking of our situation and I believe we've come up with a plan to get *The Dagger* back."

Jameson stood, brushing the sand from his clothes. He approached Edward, his voice low and menacing. "Aye. Ye said that. It could no' wait?"

Edward seemed puzzled as he scrunched up his nose and mouth while rubbing his jaw. "No. Is your ship not important to you?"

"We should go back to the others," Danielle said. She started walking back, feeling disappointed by the interruption, but in reality, she felt the ship *was* more important than a momentary fling with a woman who could disappear at any moment. She really had no idea how time travel worked. She could climb on that little dinghy with the men and something weird could happen and she'd be alone in the middle of the ocean again. The thought made her shiver.

She walked ahead of the two men, listening to their voices as they argued. Jameson wasn't about to forgive him for what he'd just done and Edward, who'd been apologetic at first, was now arguing with him.

"I doona ken why I put up with ye!" Jameson shouted.

"Ye need me. That's why!" Edward shouted back.

Jameson hurried to catch up with Danielle. He placed his hand on the small of her back and walked with her the rest of the way to the fire.

"We're sorry, Cap'n. We told him he should wait," Lynk said.

"When has Edward ever listened to anyone?" Jameson's voice was more controlled now. He was beginning to calm down.

Danielle for her part was slightly embarrassed that these men all knew what she and Jameson were up to on their walk down the beach. She was a grown woman and she could do whatever she wanted, she reminded herself. If she wanted to make love to Jameson Mackall in the sand on this beach, then she wasn't going to feel bad about it. She shook and shook sand out of her dress and when she thought she'd gotten it all there was more. How it got inside her clothing was a mystery since she'd never worn this much dress anywhere in her life. Somehow it had managed to lodge itself into places she would never have imagined and that were now making it uncomfortable for her to sit. This type of clothing was just plain wrong for rolling around on the beach.

She sat on a piece of driftwood and adjusted herself to the most comfortable position possible. If she wasn't surrounded by men, she'd have taken the darn dress off and sat here in her shift. The men all looked comfortable. Lynk had removed his shirt and was using it for a pillow. Edward was still dressed like he was going to a fancy dinner somewhere. Jameson had removed his coat and boots. Hawes and Owen had rolled up the sleeves of their shirts and removed their boots as well.

"What is this grand plan ye've come to me with?" Jameson asked.

"I thought we'd challenge MacCreary to a game of chance. *The Dagger* would be the prize. I would win, of course."

"And what are we offering him if he wins?" Jameson asked.

"I hadn't thought of that. I was expecting I would win." Edward placed a finger on his chin as he gazed up at the sky, obviously giving it some thought.

"Even if you are to win, ye must have something to entice him. Why would he take the chance of losing the ship if there were nothing to be gained by winning?"

"It would have to be something he truly wanted then," Hawes said.

Jameson sat beside Danielle as they continued the discussion. She was now pulling on her sleeves to remove the grit that somehow managed to find its way up there.

"Sand?" Jameson asked.

"Yes. It seems to be everywhere." She brushed her hand over the bodice of her dress and heard something buckle under the pressure. "I've got it!"

"Got what?" Jameson asked.

"I know what you can use to entice MacCreary." She couldn't believe she'd forgotten about the map. It would surely be of greater value to MacCreary than the ship itself.

"What would that be?" Edward asked, sounding like there was no way she could possibly have anything of value.

Danielle reached between her breasts as the men's wide-open gazes followed her hand.

"What about this?" She pulled MacCreary's treasure map from her bodice and held it out to Jameson.

"Where'd ye get this?" He unfurled it, staring thoughtfully at what he was seeing before glancing around at the men.

"I took it from MacCreary after he'd hidden it in his cabin." She was feeling pretty proud of herself at this moment.

The men were still staring this time with mouths agape. Jameson continued looking over the map.

"He didn't trust anyone on his ship, so he hid it behind some books. I guess he didn't think I'd take it."

"When he finds out 'tis gone, he'll come after ye." Jameson gazed at her with concern. It was obvious he was worried about what MacCreary might do.

"I imagine he will." Her only thought when she'd taken it was that she might be able to use it as a bargaining chip. She hadn't thought about the repercussions of angering a pirate.

"The lass is one of us. She's the heart of a pirate!" Hawes broke out in laughter and was joined by everyone but Jameson, who gazed at her with admiration, causing her to blush.

"This will definitely work, but we must protect ye from him. He'll be searching for ye."

"We will no' leave her alone, Cap'n," Lynk said.

"Once we're in St. George's ye'll stay with Lady Charlotte."

Danielle wouldn't mind that. She enjoyed Lady Charlotte's company. It would be good to see her again.

"Owen, ye say he'll be in St. George's?" Jameson asked.

"Aye, Cap'n. He's headed there now."

"I'll hold onto the map. He may try to take it from us if he sees us before we see him."

"Ye're right. He would," Hawes said.

"We'll need our rest. A good night's sleep and we'll be ready for him when the new day dawns."

Jameson rolled his jacket into a pillow and set it on the sand, motioning for Danielle to rest her head there.

"Ye're a surprising woman." He gazed at her with admiration in his eyes.

"How so?"

He caressed her cheek with his thumb. "The ways are too numerous to count."

The men found spots on the sand, making themselves as comfortable as they could. Jameson lay down beside her. She turned onto her side to face him. "Thanks for this." She indicated the rolled up jacket.

"Only the best for m'lady."

Danielle liked the sound of that. It seemed she had no control over how he felt about her. With each passing day that they were together it would be more and more difficult not to break his heart and her own if things inevitably had to come to an end.

CHAPTER 10

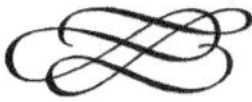

The following morning, after a choppy trip that began at sunrise and took them from the beach at Tucker's Town, they arrived at a tiny inlet just outside of St. George's. Danielle was surprised that although the waters weren't calm, she didn't suffer from any seasickness and hoped she had somehow been able to overcome it as Hawes had suggested she might.

"We'll meet tonight at the tavern by the docks," Jameson instructed the men. "In the meantime, stay out of sight."

"Aye, Cap'n," Hawes said. He, Lynk and Owen pulled the boat ashore and secured it.

"I'm coming with you," Edward announced. "I haven't seen Lady Charlotte in some time."

Jameson looked as though he might object, but instead he began walking. "We've no' far to go." He directed his comment to Danielle who walked by his side. "Perhaps ye can rest when we get there. Ye did no' sleep well last night."

"If you know that, then neither did you," she replied.

"Ye seem well. The boat did no' cause ye to feel ill?"

"Surprisingly."

"Good." He stopped for a moment to brush a windblown hair from her face. "Lady Charlotte will be happy to see ye. She'll wish to pamper ye."

"I must look terrible." She knew her hair had gone from perfectly coiffed to a tangle of knots and frizz.

"Ye look beautiful as ye always do."

His heartfelt words and the admiration in his eyes were exactly what she needed.

When they reached Lady Charlotte's home, the door was opened for them by the lady herself. "I saw you coming through my front window," she explained. "Danielle, I'm so happy to see you again. Come in, please." She looked Danielle over from head to toe. "Tsk, tsk. You are very hard on your dresses. Luckily, I've plenty for you to wear upstairs, but first you all must be hungry."

"Lady Charlotte, ye have no' greeted me." Edward smiled endearingly in her direction. "Are ye always this beautiful first thing in the morning?"

"Good day to you, Edward. I didn't see you there. Please forgive me."

Danielle kept the giggle that was about to erupt hidden behind her hand. There was no way Lady Charlotte had missed Edward. The man was a peacock and if there was anything Danielle knew about him it was that he would not allow himself to go unnoticed. Lady Charlotte had done it on purpose.

"Of course," Edward said. "I hope you don't mind my joining Jameson for a visit. It's been so long since I've seen you. I wished to pay my respects."

"Yes. Perhaps this time you'll behave yourself in my household."

"In other words, stay away from Alyce," Jameson said.

Edward had nothing to say to the reprimand he'd just received.

Danielle had briefly met Alyce on her last visit. She was a sweet young lady. Probably about nineteen or twenty years old, shy and definitely inexperienced when it came to men. Especially men like Edward.

"What did you do?" Danielle whispered to Edward as they

followed Lady Charlotte, who was escorted by Jameson, into the dining room.

"Nothing more than flattering her with a wee bit of my attention."

"You sure do think highly of yourself." Danielle wrinkled her nose at him.

He winked and smiled at her. "Aye. If I did no' why would anyone else?"

He *was* pretty full of himself. She was happy Lady Charlotte was onto him and would protect Alyce from falling under his spell. "Aren't there more experienced women in St. George's that you could lavish with your charm?"

He chuckled as he pulled out a chair for her to sit. "Jameson has always had an eye for a woman like yourself."

"I'm guessing you think that's a good thing?"

"Very."

After their meal, Lady Charlotte took Danielle upstairs to rest. Jameson was sure she'd also find her something else to wear while the dress he'd bought for her was repaired and cleaned. He and Edward went to the sitting room to discuss plans for the evening.

"How can we be sure MacCreary will be at the tavern?" Edward asked.

"If he's no' we'll send word that we wish to see him," Jameson said. "I ken the man. He will no' be able to resist the opportunity to see what we want."

"Once he knows, he could just take the map from us." Edward snapped his fingers in the air.

"Edward, do ye have no faith in our skills with gun and sword?" He pulled the map from his pocket and examined it, running his finger along the paper as he did.

"He'll have more men with him. We've just the two of us, Hawes, Lynk and Owen."

Jameson continued examining the map as he spoke. "The men aboard the Dagger will support us if need be. MacCreary will no' arrive with his entire crew. He'll have a few trusted men and no more."

"You're very sure of yourself, Jameson. I hope you're right."

He glanced up from the map, a scowl on his face. "This was yer idea, if I remember yer need to interrupt me last night."

Edward chuckled. "I was merely trying to protect Danielle's virtue."

"I let ye get away with it once. Doona test me again," Jameson growled.

"Doona be so serious. Ye ken I'm having fun with ye." Edward poured two drinks and handed one to Jameson.

"I do, but there are times when yer fun is no' wanted or appreciated."

"I'll no' do it again. What shall we do with our time?"

Jameson recognized the restlessness in Edward. He'd be more than happy to visit the local tavern, but Jameson wasn't interested. "Lady Charlotte must have some cards. Ye should practice beating MacCreary." Once he had *The Dagger* back in his possession he would take some rest here in St. George's to spend more time with Danielle. The men could take the ship out in search of treasure, but he had already found his and was determined to keep her.

The tavern by the wharf was filled with men from the ships docked in the harbor. Jameson and Edward found a table in the center of the room and waited. Hawes and the others arrived shortly after them, taking up positions around the room. Jameson was pleased to see members of *The Dagger's* crew enter a little later. They acknowledged Jameson and Edward before they too dispersed around the tavern.

Pitchers of ale were brought to the table and Jameson made sure that members of *The Dagger* crew were taken care of with pitchers of their own. The tavern was loud with the sound of male voices talking, shouting, laughing, and in some cases singing. All in all a typical night at any dockside tavern.

Jameson glanced up and nudged Edward as the door to the tavern opened and Domnhaill MacCreary and three of his men entered.

Spotting them right away, MacCreary approached their table. "What are ye doing here? When I left ye at Spanish Point I did no' expect ye to find yer way here so quickly."

"Care to join us for a drink?" Jameson asked.

"Are ye paying?" MacCreary asked.

"I'll share our drink with ye. Sit."

MacCreary pulled a chair up to the table. His men continued to stand behind him. "Why do I get the feeling there's something ye want from me?"

"There is something. I want my ship back." Jameson signaled to the barman that he needed more mugs and ale.

"We made a bargain. The ship for the lass. Have ye lost her already?" MacCreary chuckled at this and glanced behind him to his men, who also laughed.

Jameson ignored his remark. "Edward here was wondering if ye'd care to make a wager?"

"I already have yer ship. Have ye something else ye wish to give me?" Again he laughed along with his men.

"No' give, but I'm sure 'tis something ye would like to have. If Edward wins, my ship is returned. If he loses, ye keep the ship and ye'll receive this." Jameson held up the map, unfurling it so that MacCreary could see exactly what he was holding.

"Where did ye get it?" MacCreary's face turned bright red as he sputtered and fumed. "'Tis mine!"

"*Was* yers." Jameson folded the map and tucked it into his pocket.

"The lass stole it. 'Tis where ye got it. Where is she?" He craned his neck as he searched the tavern.

"Safely away from ye," Jameson said.

The mugs and ale arrived. Jameson poured a mug, placing it in front of MacCreary, who swallowed it in one long gulp. His men helped themselves.

"What do you say? Do you feel lucky?" Edward asked.

"Aye. I do." He wiped his mouth on his sleeve.

Edward pulled out a deck of cards and shuffled them in MacCreary's face.

"No' cards. Dice." MacCreary reached into his pocket and pulled out a pair of dice, placing them on the table.

Edward exchanged a glance with Jameson. "I'll no' play with yer dice."

"And I'll no' play with yer deck." MacCreary folded his arms across his chest, leaning back in his chair.

Jameson stood. "Does any man here have dice for a fair game?"

Murmurs could be heard all around them before the room went silent. A tall, bearded man who had been in the bar since they'd arrived came forward. "Aye. Ye can use these."

"Are they good dice?" Jameson asked.

"They are."

Edward leaned in to whisper to Jameson. "I'm no good with dice."

"I'll play." Jameson took the dice in his hand, weighing them and then examining each. He handed them to Domnhaill who did the same. "Clear some room."

The men cleared tables out of the way from the center of the room to the back wall.

"What's the game?" Domnhaill asked.

Jameson called to the man who owned the dice over to his side. "This man'll make a throw and we'll each take turns until we match it. Three out of five wins."

Domnhaill scratched at his beard. It was obvious that he didn't wish to risk losing *The Dagger*, but he wanted the map. He exchanged a glance with one of the men behind him who then left the tavern.

Jameson was sure the man would go back to the ship for reinforcements. If he won, Domnhaill wouldn't give up the ship or the map without a fight.

Jameson removed his coat and rolled up his sleeves. Domnhaill did the same. The other patrons of the tavern gathered in rows on either side of the area they'd cleared to roll.

Looking at the man with the dice, Jameson said, "Yer name, sir."

"Abram."

"Roll the dice, Abram."

He rolled a two. Groans could be heard all around them as it was the hardest number to roll.

"I'll go first," Domnhaill said, taking the dice from Abram. He rolled a six.

Jameson went next. Eight.

They went back and forth several times each before Jameson finally rolled a two.

The game continued on, each man winning twice. They were down to the last of it. The next throw could end it for either one of them. Jameson knew that this was a game of chance and there was every possibility that he would walk away the loser. He also knew that if he won, MacCreary's men were likely waiting outside to take the map and keep his ship. He made eye contact with Hawes who understood without words what was needed. He disappeared into the crowd, leaving Jameson to throw the dice. Abram's throw had been a seven, one of the easier throws to make. MacCreary threw a five. Jameson closed his eyes and said a silent prayer before releasing the dice to clatter against the wall. He'd thrown a seven. A cheer went up among the men of *The Dagger*.

Domnhaill cursed as he stormed toward the door. "This is no' over, Mackall."

Edward clapped Jameson on the back. "Ye did it."

"Aye, but as the man said, 'tis no' over."

Hawes pushed his way through the crowd. "The men are ready if need be and from the looks of it MacCreary's men are outside waiting."

"Is everyone armed?" Jameson said.

"Aye, Cap'n. I made sure of it."

"Men of *The Dagger*," Jameson called to those in the room. "Join me. I'll need ye to keep our ship. If ye've nothing to do with this fight, it would be best to stay inside."

They made their way to the door and taking one final look around him, Jameson pushed through and out into the alley in front of the tavern.

"I'll have me map." Domnhaill MacCreary held out his hand expecting Jameson would just hand it over to him. Surrounded by his men and seeming to believe he'd already won this battle, the smug look on his face was one Jameson would gladly help remove.

"The map is no longer yers."

"It was stolen from me. Ye received ill-gotten goods."

Jameson laughed. "Fancy words coming from the likes of ye. We had a bargain. I won. Ye lost. The map is mine. Now if ye'll clear a path." He signaled his men and they moved forward toward MacCreary and his crew. Cutlasses were drawn.

There would be no avoiding the brawl that was about to happen. Jameson signaled his men and they surged forward into the crowd. The clink of metal on metal reverberated in the narrow alleyway. Jameson faced MacCreary, who although he was older and less fit, was a very good swordsman. Jameson thanked his father for insisting that he learn to use a sword from a very early age. He, too, was a force to be reckoned with in a fight.

As the battle continued, men were dropping all around him. His crew were faring better than their opponents and had succeeded in removing most of them from the fight.

"Surrender, MacCreary. Yer numbers are no' what they were at the start of this." Jameson advanced as MacCreary moved back and got tangled up with one of his own men who had fallen. MacCreary fell backward, landing on his man and losing his cutlass.

Jameson had no intention of killing MacCreary. He signaled his men. "I'll meet ye back at the ship. Do no' allow MacCreary or his men aboard." He stepped around the fallen captain. "The next time I will no' be so generous."

"Tell yer lass I've a score to settle with her," MacCreary growled.

"If ye touch her, it will be the last thing ye ever do." It was a warning that any smart man would heed.

MacCreary laughed half-heartedly. "Doona bet on it."

"After what happened here, perhaps ye are the one who should no' bet."

Edward joined Jameson as the other men headed for *The Dagger*. They moved back-to-back through the fallen men and for a good distance until they were clear of the alley and its occupants.

"It would no' be wise to stay in port for long," Edward said.

"Aye. A day or two at best."

"Ye'll need to keep watch for MacCreary. He's not the kind to let this go." Edward took a look behind them, perhaps expecting someone to be foolish enough to follow them.

"I ken it," Jameson said.

"I've sent him off on a wild goose chase. He believes he now knows where the Spanish galleon sails," Edward chuckled.

"We could no' find them. How will he?" They'd been searching for weeks with no luck.

"He'll find the same Spanish warship we came across." Edward puffed out his chest as they walked, obviously quite proud of himself.

"Ye're a sly one." Jameson clapped him on the back.

"I offered the information to one of his men in exchange for a pitcher of ale."

Jameson laughed. "I'd hate to be the man who tells MacCreary where to find that treasure ship."

Edward joined in the laughter, checking behind them once again to be sure they weren't being followed. They took a circuitous route back to Lady Charlotte's home, not wishing to lead any trouble to her doorstep.

As they entered, there was a look of horror on Danielle's face. Lady Charlotte looked equally dismayed.

"Jameson! What happened?" Danielle said. She cautiously approached, seeming as if she didn't wish to hurt him. Her hand tentatively reached out and touched his face, which he was sure would be bruised in the morning, but now was probably red and swollen.

"MacCreary didn't take kindly to losing his map," he explained.

"You got the ship back!" Danielle threw her arms around him and then quickly let go, stepping back away from him. "I'm sorry."

"Doona be. Ye did no' hurt me."

"Or me," Edward teased.

Lady Charlotte rolled her eyes at his comment. "You'll need to get cleaned up. Edward, you can use the same room you used on your last visit. And stay away from Alyce."

"I will. I promise."

"I'll have John bring you what you need."

"Thank you, Lady Charlotte. You are a very generous woman." Despite his disheveled appearance, he bounded up the stairs.

Jameson reached into his coat and pulled out the map. "I believe this is yers." He handed it to Danielle.

"Why are you giving it to me?" she asked, not wanting to take it from him.

"Ye are the one who pilfered it. 'Tis yers. Now, if ye'll excuse me."

"Keep it safe for me," she said. "Do you need help? I'd be happy to…"

"Yes. By all means, Danielle. Help him. He doesn't know what's good for him." Lady Charlotte left them standing in the foyer.

She took his arm and guided him to his room at the top of the stairs. Jameson smiled to himself. He didn't need her help. He wasn't injured aside from a few scrapes and bruises, but she seemed so concerned about his well-being and he was enjoying it. He leaned on her, but not with his full weight. It would be wrong to take complete advantage of her kindness.

CHAPTER 11

*D*anielle took Jameson's chin in her hand, turning his head in both directions. "This one bruise on your cheek is the only thing I see."

A knock at the door brought John with a pitcher of water and some cloths. He set them down on a nearby table where Danielle soaked one of the cloths and applied it to Jameson's cheek. "A little ice would be great right about now."

Jameson tried to cock an eyebrow at this, but it only brought pain to the reddened area of his cheekbone.

"Luckily, whoever hit you missed your eye." Danielle fussed over him like a mother hen.

"I'm fine, lass. Ye needn't worry over me." A sensuous curl of his lips caused her to forget what she was doing for a moment.

"Are you hurt anywhere else?" she asked. "Maybe you should take your shirt off." Danielle was playing his game now and was pleased as he began unbuttoning it.

"I may need yer help removing it," he said.

She brushed his hands aside and finished with the buttons. Draping the shirt back over his shoulders, she ran her hands over his chest, which was strong and hard. "I don't see anything here." Her hands moved down to his abdomen which was taut and lean.

A sharp intake of breath told Danielle he liked what she was doing. "Nothing here either." She moved her hands towards the waist of his pants.

"Go no further, lass, unless ye wish me to take ye right here," he warned.

"I wanted you to take me last night on the beach, but we were interrupted." She looked behind her. "Edward's not around, is he?"

A deep chuckle rumbled from Jameson's chest. He pulled Danielle between his legs and looked up into her face. "Do ye ken what ye've started?"

"Oh, I do." She pushed him back onto the bed and lay on top of him.

His kisses were hot and passionate, his body hard in all the right places. Strong arms wrapped around her, securing her to him head to toe.

"Shall we get this dress off of ye?" A husky whisper in her ear, followed by a nibble on the lobe sent a rush of heat through her.

"Good idea." She moved off of him, stood and turned her back for his help in undoing the laces she had a love/hate relationship with.

He was an expert at undressing her. Every touch of his fingers down her spine caused her to ache in the place she really wanted to feel his caress. What was it about a man helping his woman out of her dress that was so damn sexy? Was it the anticipation of what was to come? Or was it that it was something reserved just for her and no one else?

Once undone, the dress fell to the floor, followed by her shift. Jameson's appreciation of her body was evident. He looked at her with such longing and reverence that it touched her heart. He reached for her and she went to him, allowing him to pull her close. His hands and eyes roved over her entire body, paying special attention to her breasts. He lovingly pinched her nipples, causing a moan to escape her lips before he took them into his mouth one at a time. Danielle's knees weakened, but Jameson held her steady, his hands grasping her hips.

She thrust her pelvis forward as his hand moved between her thighs to find her sensitive nub, rolling it between his fingers. She held tight to his shoulders as he kissed her belly before pulling her back down to the bed.

"Ye're so beautiful." He gazed into her eyes. Danielle saw love there and was moved by it. She caressed his cheek and then combed her fingers through his hair before kissing him, tenderly at first, but then with more urgency as her desire built.

Jameson's mouth covered hers. Slowly and with great care he continued his exploration of her body. His hands, lips and tongue found every sensitive spot and even some she didn't know could be so responsive.

Danielle did some exploring of her own, enjoying the feel and contour of his abs, his chest covered with a light sprinkling of hair. Her fingers trailed down the line of hair that led from his belly to a cock hard and ready for her. Her lips left his and kissed their way south to follow her fingers.

A long, low growl escaped Jameson as his hands grasped her head. She looked up to see him watching her. A satisfied smile appeared as she licked his shaft from bottom to top. Danielle's body was responding to him in a way she hadn't felt before. She had to have him inside of her now or she thought she might lose all control. Climbing atop him, she rocked him like the ocean swells rocked his ship. Pleasure built as he held her hips in motion; she watched the ecstasy in his eyes as their movements quickened. As they each were about to reach their climax, Jameson pulled her down and covered her mouth with his own as she called out his name, her body shuddering as wave after wave of intense pleasure overtook her.

Jameson rolled her onto her back, holding her face in his hands. He kissed her again, more gently this time, before collapsing beside her wearing a smile as wide as the Atlantic Ocean.

Sated for the moment, Danielle watched Jameson close his eyes and then admired him as he slept. She was grateful to have had this experience with him. No matter what happened, she would always have this memory of him.

The more time she spent with Jameson, the more time she wanted to spend with him. Danielle was falling in love with a pirate and that wasn't even the worst of it. She was beginning to think that if fate deemed she stay in this time, she wouldn't be sorry. Of course she'd miss Susanna and some of the creature comforts that were a part of living in the twenty-first century, but Jameson…he made it all worthwhile.

Wide awake and unable to stay in bed a moment longer, she kissed Jameson's lips. "Don't open your eyes. Sleep. I'm going to go downstairs and visit with Lady Charlotte."

Without opening his eyes, he pulled her close, taking full advantage of his strength and her willingness. "Kiss me again."

Danielle obliged and after a multitude of kisses that seemed to be turning into another round of lovemaking, she pushed at his shoulders and he released her.

"Ye worked me hard and I must rest." He flopped onto his back. "But I'll be ready for ye when ye're done with yer visit."

Sliding her hand down his chest, Danielle seriously questioned why she wanted to leave this room, but she really did want him to sleep. She had no idea how much energy was involved in a sword fight and thought if it wasn't for her, Jameson would surely have slept very soundly last night. Instead, they'd spent the night in each other's arms with little to no rest for either of them. "I'll be back. I promise."

Leaving his room and closing the door, she turned to find Lady Charlotte standing there. She was embarrassed to have been caught. This was not a time when women who weren't married were supposed to be doing what she'd been doing all night long.

"I see you spent the night with Jameson." Lady Charlotte headed down the stairs.

"I did. I'm sorry. I know that's not something that's allowed in this time."

"Don't be silly. Jameson is a handsome man and you are just what he needs. I would never say that what you've done is wrong."

"Really?" Danielle couldn't believe her ears.

"Yes. Will you join me for breakfast? I wanted to speak with you about something."

Lady Charlotte led the way into the dining room. Danielle was starving. John poured them both some tea, which she'd come to understand was a new import to the island from China by way of London.

"Do you like it here? In this time?" Lady Charlotte asked as she picked up a bit of eggs onto her fork.

"Yes. Why?" Danielle scanned the table and chose eggs, ham and bread.

"I wondered if you'd thought more about staying here."

"I don't think I have much choice in the matter."

"If you could go home, you would?"

"I've got a whole life back there." She had her business, which she had worked hard to build into a successful company. It was something she was very proud of. There was also her friend Susanna. Danielle couldn't imagine how hard this had been on her. She surely thought Danielle had drowned.

"Family, I'm sure."

"I don't have any family."

"I'm so sorry, dear."

"I've got my best friend Susanna. Or at least I hope I do. She was on the ship when I fell overboard. I'd like to know that she's all right."

"I understand. You don't know what happened to her."

"Or anyone else on the boat."

"There is a way you could go back."

Danielle's mouth opened in surprise.

"I've thought about this long and hard. At first I didn't want to say anything, but then guilt overtook me. It would be selfish of me to keep you here for Jameson's sake, even though I believe you would be so good for him."

Danielle looked down at her food, which had become less interesting to her since she'd heard what Lady Charlotte was saying. "How? How can I go back and how do you know of a way?"

Lady Charlotte inhaled deeply, closing her eyes as she did. "I know because I too have traveled through time. It's why I know the story of the Mackalls."

"Were you here in Bermuda when it happened?"

"No. I was in London where I was born and raised."

She wanted to shake the information out of Lady Charlotte, but instead clenched her hands in her lap so she wouldn't. "Does Jameson know about this?"

"No. I've never told him. My husband was the only one who knew."

"You have to tell me how it happened. Was there a green sky? Or a full moon?"

"None of those things. I was wandering through an antique shop. It was one of my favorite pastimes. I was looking for things from Britain's colonial past. Preferably something to do with the U.S. colonies." She took a moment to sip her tea before continuing. "I had been discussing with the shopkeeper my love for that time period. She asked me a simple question. Would I like to visit that time? Of course I would, I told her. It would be amazing to see it firsthand."

Danielle had lost her appetite, but knew she should eat something and so she nibbled on her breakfast as Charlotte continued on with her story.

"I began my search, but after a while I hadn't found anything that appealed to me. I was just about to leave the shop when the shop-keeper called me over and handed me an old book. She said it was from the time period I was interested in. There was no title on the cover, but it felt old to my touch. I held it in the palm of my hand and it flipped open to a page that had a beautiful illustration of a woman seated beneath a tree. She was reading a book. My eyes tried to focus on the caption beneath it, but they couldn't. I felt dizzy and faint. I'm guessing I passed out. When I woke, I was in the very same bookshop with a woman who resembled the proprietress, but she was dressed very differently."

Danielle's hand was covering her mouth. "Was it the same woman?"

"It was and she seemed quite pleased with herself. She kept saying it worked. It worked. I asked her what had worked and she told me I was in the year 1700." Charlotte was looking off into the distance as if she was reliving every detail of what had happened.

"I'd say I can't imagine how you felt, but I know all too well." Danielle remembered her own shock when she realized she was no longer in her own time.

"I thought I would faint again and almost did, but that is when my husband entered the shop. He caught me before I hit the floor."

Danielle was mesmerized by her story. She reached out a hand to lay on top of Lady Charlotte's. "Incredible."

"I took one look at Harold. Something about the sight of him put me at ease. While I'd been terrified at first, he calmed me. The woman in the shop told him I was lost, that I was from a different town and he offered to take me to his home. I glanced back at the shop woman and she smiled and shooed me away. When you come back, I'll help you get home, she said."

It was a relief to know there was a way back, but I thought I'd take the time to enjoy the time period I was so fond of. I imagined that after a few days I'd head back home." She paused to take a bite of her food.

"But you didn't." She wouldn't be here if she had.

"No. I wanted to, but when I went back to the shop the woman was gone. The proprietor had no idea what I was talking about. Said he was the only one who ever worked in the shop."

"So you had no choice but to stay." Danielle's hand was now propping up her chin. She was fully invested in this story.

"At that point, I'd already started falling in love with my husband. A short time later he told me he would be leaving for Bermuda and he wanted me to join him as his wife. I couldn't go home and what could be better than spending the rest of my life with the man I loved?" The smile on Charlotte's face held both sadness and happiness, if that were possible.

"I guess you're trying to tell me I'm stuck here and I should make the best of it."

"Not quite. There's a woman here on the island. Her name is Morwenna. She's told me she could send me back to my own time whenever I like." Charlotte seemed to be examining her face for a reaction.

"Why haven't you gone?" Danielle was truly puzzled.

"When Harold died, I thought it would be best for me to leave. After all, he was what had kept me here all these years." She smiled at Danielle. "I realized he wasn't the only thing keeping me here and though he was no longer with me, there were many reasons for me to stay. This is my home now. I love it here. The island, the people, my nephew. I'd be as out of place there as I was when I first arrived in this time."

"Do you think this Morwenna would help me?" Danielle asked

Charlotte placed her napkin on the table and signaled John to take her plate. "If it's what you truly want."

"It is." She was about to say, *but I think I need more time to figure things out,* but they were interrupted before she could get the words out.

"You wish to leave?" Jameson stood in the doorway. His voice was cold and without emotion.

"Jameson, I…" She could see the look of hurt on his face, even if she couldn't hear it in his voice. She regretted saying the words she knew were at the heart of it. He expected her to stay with him, although neither of them had spoken of it. Until this very moment, she'd thought she had no choice. That this would be her life. Now she had a choice and it was the most difficult one she'd ever had to make.

"I've my ship to see to. I left the men in charge last night. MacCreary was angry. I must be sure he did no' try to steal her." He turned on his heel and left. The sound of the door closing told her he was gone.

Lady Charlotte said nothing, but she didn't have to. Her face said it all. She was disappointed and most of all sad for Jameson.

"I wish he hadn't heard that." Danielle could cry at her own reckless words.

"Perhaps it was best that he heard it straight from your mouth instead of later from me."

Danielle didn't agree. If she just disappeared, he wouldn't know that it had been because she had wanted to go. "Will you take me to this woman?"

"I will tell you where to find her." Charlotte stood to leave.

"I'd like to go today." She didn't wish to cause Jameson any more anguish. The sooner she was gone, the better.

"Finish your breakfast. I will have my carriage take you. It can only go so far and then you'll have to walk the rest of the way." There was disappointment in her voice, or was Danielle just imagining it? "John, have my carriage prepared. Miss York will be leaving us."

She couldn't choke down the rest of her breakfast. Feeling deflated and saddened by what had happened. Last night she'd been happy to be Jameson's woman. The pirate life seemed exciting to her, but when it came right down to it, going home had sounded better. It might be her only chance and she had to take it.

The carriage was waiting for her outside. Lady Charlotte walked her to the door. "The carriage will wait for you to return in case Morwenna isn't there."

"Why wouldn't she be there?" Danielle wondered. She wanted to go now. Today. She couldn't face Jameson again after what he'd heard her say.

"She comes and goes." Charlotte motioned to John, who helped Danielle into the carriage. "I've enjoyed having you here. Don't worry about Jameson. It will take time, but he will fine."

Danielle watched as Charlotte went back into the house. She didn't think she could possibly feel any worse about herself than she did at this moment. She'd hurt Jameson, which was the one thing she hadn't wanted to do, and she'd disappointed Charlotte, who must have imagined her story would have a different effect on Danielle's decision. Instead it had given her one more thing to contemplate. What if something happened to Jameson? The thought distressed her. He was a pirate after all. Could she survive in this time on her own...without him?

The carriage stopped at the end of the road. The rest of her walk was through the sand to a small cottage on the beach. She stood outside for a long while pondering whether or not she should go in. Her hesitation gave her time to think. She weighed the pros and cons in her mind. The pro column was occupied by Jameson, but it was outweighed by all of the cons. MacCreary had it in for her, so he was in the con column followed by pirates, ships, no phones or computers, no Susanna and no business. She thought about all the hard work that had gone into building her business and how excited she and Susanna were this past year when it seemed everything they touched turned to gold. It was the hardest decision of her life, but it had to be done.

Danielle knocked on the door and waited. Jameson's face floated through her mind. This could be the biggest mistake of her life, but it might also be her last chance to get back home.

CHAPTER 12

*D*isappointed and confused when Morwenna didn't answer the door, Danielle headed back toward the carriage. At least she'd be able to explain herself to Jameson, if he even wanted to see her again. As she rounded the corner of the tiny beach house, she came face-to-face with Domnhaill MacCreary.

"Just the lass I was searching for." He held a blunderbuss in his hand and it was pointed right at her.

Her stomach dropped at the sight of him. Danielle hid her shaking hands in the folds of her dress.

"Did ye no' find the hag?" he asked.

Lady Charlotte hadn't called the woman a hag, but it must be who he was referring to. "No. She wasn't home."

"Ye'll be coming with me then." He moved toward her, getting closer than she would have liked.

She did her best to dodge him, but he blocked her path. "There's a carriage waiting for me down the beach."

"He'll be waiting a long time." He whistled and two of his men appeared behind her, each taking one of her arms. "Mackall will want ye back. This time I'll get his ship and me map."

"He won't want me back." After this morning she doubted he'd ever want to have anything to do with her again.

MacCreary motioned for the men to start walking and he followed along behind with the gun to Danielle's back. "Why? What have ye done?"

She didn't have a good answer for him. At least not one he'd believe. "He's angry with me." She glanced over her shoulder to look at him.

"I doona believe ye. Any pirate who gives up his boat for a lass is well and good in love." As he said the words, his eyes crossed and he stuck his tongue out.

"Is that what you think someone in love looks like?" she questioned.

"Doona test me, lass. Yer a thief. Do ye ken what happens to thieves in these parts?" His tone was ominous.

She didn't think she wanted to know, but said, "No. I don't."

"Ye could lose one of yer pretty hands. 'Twould be a shame. If Mackall refuses to save ye, 'twill be yer fate."

She couldn't feel her feet beneath her anymore. She continued moving, so she knew they were working, but the fear coursing through her had numbed her from head to toe. She willed herself to keep going. Being strong was something she was normally good at. It was how she'd become a successful businesswoman in her own time. She cursed the fact that the woman she'd come to see hadn't been home. If she had been, Danielle might be on her way back to her own time at this very moment.

They skirted the road where the carriage sat.

"Doona even think about calling out," Domnhaill growled.

Escape was the one thing on her mind. She had to find a way, but nothing seemed to present itself. They walked down the beach to a skiff that would take them to the ship she had hoped she'd never see again.

Jameson checked on *The Dagger*, and, pleased that it was still there and his crew was completely in control, he walked back to Lady Charlotte's. He'd made up his mind. He'd be leaving today. He'd collect Edward and head back to the boat. It was clear Danielle was done with him. He thought he'd seen something that wasn't there. He'd been imagining she might love him the way he had come to love her. It would do him no good to think about it. It wasn't meant to be.

"Jameson, you're back," Lady Charlotte greeted him from the drawing room.

"No' for long. I'll be heading out as soon as I get Edward." Right now the only thought he had was to get as far away from here as he possibly could and back to what he did best.

"He was still sleeping when I checked on him earlier. I'll send John to rouse him." Charlotte rang her bell and John appeared. "Wake Mr. Sutherland, please."

John disappeared up the stairs.

"I'm sorry about Danielle," Charlotte said.

"As am I." He raked his hand through his hair, doing his best to blot out the memory of her in his arms last night.

Charlotte's eyes were filled with what could only be pity. "She went to visit the witch who lives on the beach. She hasn't returned."

"Does that mean she's gone?" He knew the answer. There was really no need to ask the question. The woman who'd looked like a drowned rat when he first saw her had transformed into a beautiful swan and over the short time he'd known her, Jameson couldn't help himself. He'd fallen in love.

Charlotte was speaking to him, but he hadn't heard a word she said. She'd obviously been telling him that Danielle was gone. That she'd left him. He didn't think his heart could hurt any more than it already did, but he was wrong. It was as though a knife had been plunged deep inside, draining him of any happiness he had left.

"Edward!" he called up the stairs.

"Coming!" Edward bounded down the stairs. "Are we going?"

"Aye. The men are waiting."

"When will you be back?" Charlotte asked, grabbing his arm before he could walk away.

"I'll try no' to be gone too long." She was one of the few things he could count on and she held a special place in his heart.

"Good. You know I miss you when you're away." Her lips turned up in a sad, little smile.

Jameson leaned down to kiss her cheek. She took his hand, holding it until he turned for the door. "Take care of yerself."

"And ye do the same."

Jameson and Edward headed for the wharf.

"Where are we off to?" Edward asked in his usual man-without-a-care-in-the-world tone.

"We're in search of treasure." Jameson kept a good pace as they reached the wharf area.

"MacCreary's treasure?" Edward asked.

"We've got the map. What else would we do?" He broke into a jog and Edward did the same.

"His ship is still in port," Edward noted as they spotted it where it had been moored in the harbor. "I would have thought he'd be on his way to find Spanish gold."

"Mayhap they needed a day to recover from the beating they were given last night," Jameson snarled.

"Speaking of last night. I thought Danielle would be joining us." Edward broached the subject as if he knew something was amiss.

"She will no'." Jameson's reply was short and to the point.

"Why, might I ask?"

"Ye may no'." He gave Edward a fierce stare that told him to mind his own business.

Edward held up his hands in surrender. "Fine."

The ship was ready to sail. The men had restocked food, water and other essentials they'd need for their voyage. Once Jameson and Edward were aboard, they were on their way.

They passed *The Savage Wolf* as they left the harbor. Jameson wondered what exactly MacCreary was up to. His men were readying the ship. He hoped they'd be heading to different ports, but MacCreary might very possibly try to follow him. He wasn't going to give up the treasure easily. He'd said as much the night before.

"Keep watch for MacCreary. I doona trust the man," Jameson said.

"Aye, Cap'n. I'll see to it." Hawes hurried off to have a word with one of the men.

Edward clapped him on the back. "I'll need the map if I'm to chart our course."

Jameson reached into his coat, extracting the map and handed it to Edward. "I'll be in my cabin."

Once there, he sat with his feet on the desk and a scowl on his face. He was doing his best not to think about Danielle, but he wasn't having much success. He closed his eyes and her face appeared as it had the night before. The look of rapture she'd worn as he'd pleasured her, her creamy skin soft beneath his hands, her lips scorching a path down his belly to... His hand slammed down on the desk. "Damn her!"

Swinging his legs down from the desk, he stood and began pacing angrily back and forth in front of his desk. If he couldn't get the woman out of his head, this was going to be a long and torturous voyage.

A knock at the door mercifully saved him from himself. "Come in," he shouted.

"We've set our course. I thought ye'd want to see the map." Edward entered accompanied by another man, closing the door behind him.

"Set it here." Jameson indicated the desk.

Unrolling the map, Edward put it in place with paperweights he found on the desk.

The two men carefully examined the map. "We doona ken what isle this is, but Samuel had an idea of which it *might* be." Samuel Warren was the ship's cartographer. He could read any map put before him.

"Well..." Jameson's patience was in short supply this morning.

"This is the isle we seek." Samuel pointed to a tiny speck on the top half of the map. The bottom was a map of the actual island itself and the possible treasure site. "Ye see the series of islands alongside. I believe this large one to be San Salvador."

Jameson examined the map more carefully, tracing the outline of the island with his finger. "Ye could be right."

Edward had been leaning on the desk and glanced up at Jameson. "Could be?"

"We'll see, won't we." Jameson rolled the map, tied it with a leather thong and handed it Samuel. "See that we stay on course."

"Aye, Cap'n." Samuel tucked the map under his arm and left them.

"We'll find it. I know we will." Edward sounded confident, but his face and voice softened as he looked at Jameson. "What troubles ye, friend?"

Jameson gazed up at the ceiling, hands on his hips.

"Do ye regret leaving Danielle behind?" Edward asked.

"No' at all," he lied.

"Then why do ye look like a man who has lost a greater treasure than the one we seek?" Edward sat on the edge of Jameson's desk.

"Edward, I will never understand women." Jameson's gaze moved from the ceiling to focus on his friend.

"Who can? They are a great mystery, but one always worth exploring."

"I'm no' so sure." Perhaps he would be better off seeking his relief with the women in the ports they frequented whom he had no attachment to.

"What happened?" Rather than the normal prodding Edward was inclined to use on Jameson, he sounded as if he actually cared.

"I doona ken. I thought I understood her, but I was wrong." He was a man who knew what he wanted and had never had any trouble getting it. He was confused by her seeming indifference. Had she been putting on a performance for his benefit?

Edward hopped off of the desk and pulled a chair up and sat. "Even Abigail did no' have this effect on ye."

"Because I did no' really love her."

"Ye've known Danielle a short time. Are ye sure?"

Jameson dropped his head to his chest as he spoke. "Love does no' follow the rules of time. It happens as it wishes."

"Then I am truly sorry." Removing a flask from his coat, Edward took a long pull.

"Doona worry for me. I will be fine. We've a treasure to find." He would focus on the treasure. It was always something that could take his mind off of any troubles he may be experiencing. The challenge of the search and the thrill of discovery held him in its thrall.

"Drink?" He offered Jameson the flask.

"No. I wish to keep my head clear, as should ye."

The flask was tucked away once again. "Aye, Cap'n."

D anielle couldn't believe she was aboard *The Savage Wolf* again. She had horrible luck, it seemed. She regretted leaving Lady Charlotte's home that morning. She regretted that Jameson had heard her saying she wanted to go back home. She really regretted running into Domnhaill MacCreary. Hindsight was twenty-twenty, as they said. All of the *if onlys* meant nothing in her current situation. She was in the custody of a murderous pirate who hadn't harmed her yet, but she'd really angered him when she stole his map and that was very clear. She felt that at any moment if things didn't go the way he wanted, she could find herself overboard or minus a hand or both.

The ship was on course to follow *The Dagger*, with the intent of overtaking it as it approached the treasure, which Domnhaill was assuming was the ship's destination. Danielle couldn't imagine why Jameson would be interested in saving her a third time, but she hoped he wasn't the kind of man who held a grudge. If only she'd met him in her own time things would be different. He wasn't the type of man she'd easily let slip through her fingers as she'd done this time.

She scanned the cabin in search of something, anything that might be her salvation. MacCreary made sure to remove anything that she might use as a weapon and his important papers were now all locked in a chest he'd placed on board the ship in St. George's.

The door flew open and an angry Domnhaill MacCreary entered. "Damn them all!" he shouted.

"What's wrong?" She was trying to stay on his good side, so seeming concerned for him was her goal.

"Me men do no' wish to battle with Mackall." He stormed through the cabin to his desk where he pounded his fist on the desk before plopping into his chair.

"You're the captain. Don't they have to do what you want?" she asked.

"They can vote to overrule me. 'Tis the way of a pirate ship."

"I didn't know that."

"Well, now ye do and ye should ken that if we doona go after Mackall, I'll be exacting me revenge."

"On me?" The jeopardy she was in became even clearer.

"Aye, little lass. On ye."

"Well, then we'd better find a way to get them to do what you want."

Domnhaill narrowed his eyes into a scowl. "How would ye do that?"

"I know something that might be of interest to them." She thought quickly of the research she'd done on pirates before the cruise. If she could convince him she knew where another treasure was located, then perhaps she could buy herself more time.

"What would that be?" If there was a picture of suspicious in the dictionary, Domnhaill MacCreary would be it.

"I know where Blackbeard's treasure is buried," she blurted out.

MacCreary was around the desk in a flash, grabbing her by the arm. "How would ye ken it?"

She wrenched her arm free and rubbed it where his fingers had wrapped around it like a vice. "There's something about me that you don't know."

"Aye. Keep talking."

"I'm from another time and because I am, I know all about your treasure and the treasure of many other pirates." Danielle wasn't sure he believed her. He was staring at her and not saying a thing, but she could tell that the wheels were turning. She'd either just won him over or signed her own death certificate.

"Why should I believe ye?" he growled.

So far, his bark had been worse than his bite. At least he wasn't totally discounting what she'd just said. "I probably know a lot of things about the future that you don't. Like, for instance, the colonies are going to revolt against the king in 1776 and become their own country."

"Ye went to the hag to help ye. Why?"

"I wanted to go back home. I was told she could make that happen."

"If I believed ye, and I'm no' sure that I do, tell me what do ye ken about me?"

She didn't know anything, but thought it best to make up a fantastic story that would impress him. "In my time, you are quite famous. You became a very wealthy man. After pirating turned into a very dangerous business you were smart enough to take your treasure and buy yourself an estate in Jamaica where you lived to be a very old man. There's even a statue in your honor."

He was nodding in agreement. "I've always loved Jamaica."

Nothing she'd told him was true, but it had done exactly what she hoped it would do. She'd flattered his ego. Hopefully that was enough to keep her alive. "Part of the reason you became so wealthy was the treasure. You have to get the map back." If he accepted what she was telling him, she should be able to get to Jameson. She felt guilty encouraging Domnhaill to go after him, but it seemed that his men had been soundly beaten by the crew of *The Dagger* the last time they met in St. George's and they weren't interested in a rematch. With any luck, the results would be the same. Jameson was her only hope of getting out of this situation with both hands and her life.

"Aye. If only ye hadn't taken it from me," he grumbled.

"I apologize. It was wrong of me, but the thought of finding all that gold..." She glanced at him before lowering her eyes and examining her hands. The ones she was planning on keeping. "I guess I don't have to tell you about the lure of gold."

"Nay. Ye doona, lass. I'll speak with the men again. I only need one or two more on me side."

She breathed a sigh of relief as he left her. This plan of hers had better work because making Domnhaill angrier with her than he already was would be the end of her.

CHAPTER 13

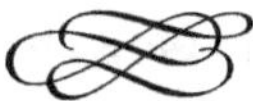

Three days after setting sail from St. George's, *The Dagger* had just passed the island of San Salvador. If they were right, the isle they sought wasn't far.

"We should see the isle soon, I believe," Edward said, joining Jameson on the quarterdeck.

Jameson handed him his spyglass. "I'm no' seeing another isle. We could be wrong about the location."

"'Tis possible. We'll know soon."

Edward, who never missed an opportunity to harass Jameson, had been taking it easy on him and he knew why. His friend pitied him. In fact, he pitied himself. He'd spent the last three days pining for a woman who would never be his. He wondered where she was, what she was doing and if some other man was kissing her at this very moment. The thought of it brought him more pain than he'd thought possible. Parting from other women had never hit him with such force, even Abigail whom he thought he loved. It was only after meeting Danielle that he realized how wrong he'd been.

"Where have ye gone?" Edward was asking him.

"No' far."

"Good because I believe I see our island on the horizon."

Jameson took the spyglass and pointed in the direction Edward indicated. "Aye. It won't be long now."

The men of *The Dagger* skillfully sailed the ship as close as possible without hitting the reef skirting the beach. Skiffs were lowered and Jameson took his most trusted crew members with him onto the island. Samuel, who was accompanying them onto the island, had traced a copy of the map onto a sheet of parchment that Jameson folded and placed inside of his coat. The original was safely locked in the chest he kept in his cabin.

The skiffs were guided onto the beach, where the men pulled them ashore. They gathered their equipment and followed Jameson, Edward and Samuel as they made their way onto the sand.

"What are we looking for?" Jameson asked.

"There's a path off of the beach, where three palm trees are growing verra close together." Samuel shaded his eyes with his hands as he scanned the beach.

They glanced around and found groups of palms everywhere they looked.

"I doona see three trees together," Jameson said.

"Over there," Edward said, pointing to a spot farther down the beach.

In the midst of several other trees, there stood three that were particularly close together.

They began walking toward the grouping when one of the crew called out. "Cap'n Mackall. There's another ship."

Jameson turned to see *The Savage Wolf* weighing anchor beside *The Dagger*. "Damn him." MacCreary had managed to stay just far enough away that they hadn't seen him.

"Should we go back to the ship?" Edward asked.

"No. The treasure is what he wants. He'll take *The Dagger* if possible, but the crew will stand guard." Jameson knew his men. They wouldn't give up the ship without a fight and he was sure they'd win.

"He has us at a disadvantage," Samuel said, shielding his eyes to block the sun glinting off the water.

"My guess is he'll be joining us on the beach. We'll wait here for him." Jameson folded his arms across his chest and kept his eye on *The Savage Wolf*

His men were all well-armed and Jameson was sure that in a battle they would be victorious, just as they had been outside of the tavern.

As he expected, skiffs were launched from MacCreary's ship and headed their way. They stood their ground as he approached the beach. Jameson used his spyglass to assess those in the boats. "I doona believe it!"

"What? What is it?" Edward asked, obviously straining his eyes to see.

"She's with him. Danielle is on the skiff with MacCreary." How had she ended up with him again and more importantly why hadn't she returned to her own time?

"That lass has a way of finding trouble, does she not?" Edward plucked a piece of beach grass which he twirled in his fingers before placing it between his lips.

"I would say she does." Things had just gotten a lot more complicated than they'd been a few moments ago. MacCreary knew his weakness and was willing to take full advantage of it. He also knew she'd given Jameson the map and he'd threatened revenge on her for her actions.

"Go no farther, Mackall!" MacCreary hopped over the side of the boat and splashed his way toward the shore. "'Tis me treasure ye seek. The lass told me so."

Jameson exchanged an amused glance with Edward, but the amusement immediately left his face when he saw Danielle being dragged from the skiff and onto the beach by two of MacCreary's men. She looked shaken and afraid.

"Has he harmed ye?" Jameson asked as she got closer.

"Not yet," she assured him as she wrestled herself free of the two men.

"Ye can no' have me treasure. The lass tells me that she kens I am to be a wealthy man and that this treasure will make it so." MacCreary's glance spanned everyone on the beach as if challenging them to disagree with what they'd just heard.

Jameson sent her a questioning look. "Is that true?"

Danielle looked from him to MacCreary and back again, shrugging her shoulders.

"Did ye lie to me, lass?" MacCreary turned sharply in her direction.

Danielle gazed at Jameson. Her eyes seemed to plead with him. "I'm sorry. I told him he needed the treasure. It was the only way I could get to you."

"Are ye telling me ye were willing to put my men at risk to save yerself?" This woman had stolen a map, stolen his heart and seemed to have no end to the lengths she would go to save her own skin. He had to admire her creativity.

"I know. It's bad, but I didn't know what to do. He was going to cut my hand off or worse." She held one up to show him.

"And I will do, now," MacCreary snarled.

Jameson glared at him. "Ye lay a hand on her, MacCreary, and it will be the last thing ye ever do."

MacCreary held up his hands apparently thinking to calm him. "I'll no' harm her if ye give me the map and show me where the treasure is."

"There is no treasure here," Jameson said. "The clues on the map were no' found."

"So ye say. I doona believe ye."

"We've only just landed. Since ye've been following us, I'm sure ye ken it. We have no' had time to search, but I can tell ye the first clue is no' to be found."

"Hand over the map." MacCreary grabbed hold of Danielle's hand at the wrist, holding his blade above it.

A small shriek escaped Danielle as she tried to pull her wrist free.

"Give me the lass." Jameson's voice was low and ominous.

They eyed each other with suspicion. Jameson didn't trust the man and he was sure the feeling was mutual.

A loud boom from offshore caused them all to stop what they were doing and face the water. A Spanish warship was slicing through the water toward both ships and firing its cannons as it approached.

"To the boat," MacCreary shouted. He grabbed Danielle by the arm, but she kicked him in the shins. He let go of her and hopped a few steps before trying to retrieve her.

Jameson was faster. He scooped Danielle up into his arms and headed for his skiff. "There's yer map, MacCreary." He dropped it on the sand where several of MacCreary's men dove after it. It wouldn't give them much time, but enough to make it back to *The Dagger* before MacCreary and his men could reach *The Savage Wolf*.

The warship hadn't hit either boat to this point, but they continued firing. Once at the ship, Jameson tossed Danielle over his shoulder before climbing the rope ladder. "Hold on!"

Edward was right behind him. "We meet again, Danielle." He chuckled as they reached the deck and the men began lifting the skiffs.

"Weigh anchor and prepare to sail," Jameson called. "Danielle, to my cabin."

Surprisingly, she didn't say a word as she hurried across the deck and up the stairs that led to his cabin. Another volley from the Spanish cannons left the air smelling of sulfur as clouds of smoke wafted over the deck.

"They're getting closer. We've got to get out of here!" Edward called to Jameson.

The crew were all hard at work hoisting the anchor and readying the sails. In another moment, they were moving and luckily the winds were on their side. They slipped past *The Savage Wolf*, where Jameson saw MacCreary just now getting on deck. If luck remained on their side, the Spanish warship would focus on the ship left behind rather than take chase. *The Dagger* now raced through the water at a pace that would outrun the Spanish ship in no time. In their wake, the Spanish ship was indeed heading straight for *The Savage Wolf*. They would either capture the ship or destroy it. MacCreary didn't stand a chance.

"That was close," Edward said. He was now standing at Jameson's side. "It's good that MacCreary showed up when he did."

"Why do ye say that?"

"We would have been farther inland searching for the treasure and would no' have been aware of the Spanish until it was too late."

"We should be thankful then." Jameson leaned on the rail.

"Ye should go speak with the lass," Edward said.

"What's been done can no' be repaired." Jameson walked toward the center of the deck. He'd always considered himself a strong man, but at this moment he didn't have the strength to deal with the woman occupying his cabin.

"Ye can no' hold it against her. She only did what she had to do to save herself. Any of us would do the same."

"Would we? I question whether I would betray my shipmates to save my own skin."

"Aye, but she's no' a pirate, is she?"

"Danielle may be more of a pirate than any of us." She'd stolen his heart, hadn't she?

"Ye love the lass. Tell her." Edward poked him in the chest with his finger.

"What good will it do me?" On any other day, Edward would never have gotten away with prodding him, but today he didn't have it in him to retaliate.

"There's no telling, if ye doona act." Edward patted him on the shoulder before leaving him to think, which was exactly what he did not want to do. He'd done nothing *but* think since the last time he saw Danielle and it had left him in a very dark place. Seeing her again should have lifted his spirits, given him hope and touched his heart, but instead it left him with a hollow feeling that weighed him down.

"We're in the clear, Cap'n." Hawes stood before him, a large grin on his face, which disappeared quickly as he apparently read Jameson's mood. "'Tis good, aye?"

"Verra good." Jameson reassured him with what was going to have to pass for a smile, but looked more like a grimace.

"Cap'n?" Hawes questioned. "Is all well?"

"Aye. I've some business to attend to and I'm debating my position."

"Can I be of help, sir?"

"Nay, Hawes. 'Tis kind of ye to ask, but I will handle it." He couldn't avoid her forever. He should at least hear her out. "I'll be in my cabin if ye need me. Set a course for Manta Cay."

"Aye Cap'n."

Danielle made herself as comfortable as possible. Her nerves were frazzled. Between Jameson, MacCreary and now the Spanish warship, she wasn't sure how much more she could take.

The sound of the door to the cabin opening had her spinning around to see who was there. "Jameson." Breathless at the sight of him, she could do nothing more than whisper his name.

He closed the door, walking past her to his desk. "I wasn't expecting to see ye again." His voice was gruff and his words to the point.

"I know. I have to apologize about what happened. I was going to talk to you about my decision, but you left and I didn't get a chance. The last thing I wanted to do was hurt you."

He was ignoring her as he rifled through the papers on his desk. It was obvious he wasn't really looking at them.

"Did you hear me?" she asked. "I said I was sorry."

"And ye wish me to forgive ye." He glanced up at her and what she saw in his eyes told her he wouldn't.

"That would be nice, but I understand if you can't." It would be much more than nice. It would mean the world to her. It would wash away the guilt she was feeling for hurting him even if it hadn't been her intention. She should have been more clear in her intentions, but she'd let her heart guide her and that it seems had gotten her into a whole lot of trouble.

"Edward tells me that I should let ye ken how I feel. That I should tell ye I love ye, but what good would it do?" He still was avoiding making eye contact with her.

Danielle stood at attention. "Did you just say you loved me?"

He didn't answer her. Instead he closed his eyes and inhaled deeply.

"Because I've fallen in love you with you, too. I didn't want to and I certainly didn't think it was possible in such a short time, but I have. I wanted to tell you, but I never got the chance." Danielle moved toward him, hoping he would take her in his arms, but he stood still, not welcoming her into his embrace.

"It would do neither of us any good to continue on. Ye will leave as soon as the opportunity arises, will ye no'?"

"I don't know if I can leave. The woman Charlotte told me about wasn't home when I got there."

"Ye *want* to leave. That is what I know and that is why ye and I canno' be."

Danielle was crushed and confused. He was right. What had she been thinking? She couldn't ask him to love her and then expect he wouldn't be hurt when she left him. "You're right. I can't do that to you. You're a good man. You've saved me *three* times now. And this last time I didn't deserve your help."

He took in another deep breath, and his dark, soulful eyes penetrated straight through to her heart. There was nothing she could do with the overwhelming feelings she had for Jameson. Even if she stayed. Even if she wanted to, he would not put himself in a position to let himself love her ever again. It was clear to Danielle, she'd really messed things up.

CHAPTER 14

Standing on deck as *The Dagger* approached the harbor of Manta Cay, Danielle was taken by the beauty of the island. The turquoise water was so clear she could see far into its depths. The harbor was busy, much as St. George's and Charleston had been, and she couldn't wait to get ashore and away from *The Dagger*'s brooding captain. He told her she would be staying with his uncle Rourke Mackall and his wife, Lizette.

Rourke was the governor of the island, which surprised her because Edward told her that he'd been a pirate beforehand.

"Secure the ship," Jameson called to his crew. The men scrambled around the deck obeying his order.

Edward, on the other hand, remained by her side. "I'll be escorting ye to the governor's home."

"Isn't Jameson going to see his uncle?" she asked. If he was trying to avoid her, this was going above and beyond.

"He'll visit later. He has business here on the island," Edward explained.

She wanted to ask what business, but did it really matter?

The ship came to a stop and after a few moments; skiffs were lowered. Edward took her arm and helped her over the side where one of the men guided her down and aided her as she boarded. She sat in the center of the boat as she'd done the day she'd been rescued. Edward joined her as the men began rowing the skiff ashore.

There was a small segment of beach near the piers and this was where they grounded the small boat. Edward took her hand so she could stand. He hopped over the side into the water and lifted her into his arms, carrying her to a dry spot in the sand where he put her down. "This way." He motioned as she followed along beside him.

"This is all so strange," she said, feeling completely at a loss.

"Doona fear, he'll come around." Edward slowed his pace so she could keep up with him.

She hadn't been talking about Jameson, but it appeared Edward had something to say. "Do you think so? He seems pretty angry with me."

"I doona believe angry to be the right word. Confused…yes, confused."

"About what?" Danielle knew there were a million reasons for him to be confused, but was curious to hear Edward's viewpoint on the subject.

"Ye, of course. He gave ye his heart and with little thought ye tore it apart."

"I wouldn't say with little thought. I didn't want to hurt him, Edward."

"Ye did no' mean to, but ye did. Perhaps I should have said with no thought."

The pain his words gave her went straight to her heart, which was already heavy with regret, guilt and despair. "And what can I do to fix it?" Danielle would take any help she could get at this point.

He turned his head to look at her. "Patience, m'dear. Continue to be yer beautiful, charming self. Ignore his moodiness. He'll be yours again, have no fear."

She did have fear, and lots of it, too. There was no doubt in her mind that she loved him, and he loved her. He'd told her he did and she'd been overjoyed to know it. Danielle was so confused about so many things. She couldn't stop herself from loving him, but she also wanted to go home. Life had been so much less complicated in her own time. Edward was right. Being patient would be important.

They walked along a rutted path toward a large home surrounded by palm trees. An older man greeted them as they approached.

"Guyton," Edward said. "It's been so long since I've last seen ye. How are ye?"

"Good, sir. Happy to see you again." The man bowed slightly at the waist.

"This is Danielle York. She is a friend of Captain Mackall. Jameson Mackall, that is." He laughed and then explained to Danielle. "Rourke was the captain of *The Dagger*, ye ken."

"Mrs. Mackall will be happy to meet you, miss."

"That would be Lizette. Her father was the governor of the island and a good friend of Rourke."

"Does he still live here?" she asked.

"Nay. He was murdered by a loathsome man, several years ago."

Danielle's hand flew to her mouth. How tragic for Lizette to lose her father that way. They were led into a large foyer on the main floor of the house.

"This way, please." Guyton led them into a drawing room that was beautifully furnished. It rivaled Lady Charlotte's home in Bermuda. "Have a seat. I will let the Miss Lizette know ye are here."

"This is beautiful," Danielle said to Edward after Guyton had left them. The chairs, tables and curtains looked similar to the rooms she'd seen displayed at the art museum in New York.

"Good morning." A petite blonde woman, who Danielle assumed was Lizette Mackall, entered the room.

"Lizette, 'tis good to see you again," Edward said, he took her hand and bent to kiss it. "May I introduce ye to Danielle York."

Lizette tipped her head to the side, acknowledging Danielle. "Edward, I didn't know you were married."

Danielle almost burst into laughter as Edward stumbled over himself to explain. "No, no, no. This is not my wife."

Lizette looked from Edward to Danielle, awaiting an explanation.

Danielle was doing the same. She couldn't wait to hear how Edward explained her.

"Danielle is a friend of Jameson's. She had some difficulties with Domnhaill MacCreary and we rescued her."

"How terrible." Lizette's voice was sympathetic as she turned to Danielle. "You must have been quite frightened."

"I hope I never see the man again," Danielle said.

"With Jameson as your protector, I do not think you will."

Little did Lizette know that Jameson wanted nothing to do with Danielle and she couldn't even be sure he wouldn't just leave her here in Manta Cay to fend for herself.

"Speaking of Jameson, where is he?" Lizette asked.

"He had some business in town. I'm sure he'll be here shortly."

"Rourke is in town, as well. Perhaps their business is the same." She indicated that they should sit. "Will you be staying with us?"

"I believe Danielle will be staying. I will stay in town at the inn."

"Nonsense. You will stay here with us," Lizette insisted. "We've plenty of room."

Danielle listened to the conversation with great interest. It was obvious Edward wanted the freedom to do whatever it was he did when he wasn't aboard the ship. "I could no' impose on yer kindness."

Lizette was enjoying Edward's discomfort. That much was obvious. It seemed she had a lot in common with Lady Charlotte. Edward was a lovable character. Much too good looking and obviously a ladies' man. He was the male version of her best friend Susanna.

The back and forth continued between Lizette and Edward, with Lizette finally allowing him to have his way. "I'll have Maria make us some tea." She left the room.

"What's so bad about staying here?" Danielle asked.

"Nothing at all. 'Tis a lovely place, but I fear I'd be bored." Edward picked up a small box from one of the tables, examining it before he replaced it.

"You'd be perfect for my friend Susanna." She'd thought this more than once since she met Edward.

She'd piqued his interest. "Is she as pretty as ye?"

"Prettier."

"When can I meet her?" He seemed excited at the prospect.

"You can't." She felt a little, tiny bit bad she'd gotten his hopes up.

"Then why tease me with the thought of her." His disappointment was showing.

"No reason. I was just thinking about her and how much like you she is."

He scrunched his eyebrows. "A female version of me?"

"Exactly."

"I must meet her."

"Good luck with that. She's far away from here."

Lizette returned. "Join me in the dining room."

Danielle and Edward followed her into a lovely dining room containing a beautiful mahogany table and chairs. The seats were a beautiful floral brocade. The tea set and tray were set at one end where three cups had been placed along with a selection of sweet cakes, fruit and cheese.

"Please, help yourselves." Lizette sat at the end of the table, Danielle to her right and Edward to her left.

"Everything looks delicious," Danielle said.

Lizette filled a cup with tea and handed it to Edward. She filled another for Danielle before pouring one for herself. "Maria is a very good cook. We have a beautiful garden and she grows many fruits and vegetables. I can guarantee you that the meals you eat here will far surpass what's available on board *The Dagger*." It was apparent that Lizette was very proud of her household and it seemed rightfully so.

Edward was becoming more and more distracted, which was noted not only by Danielle, but also Lizette.

"Edward, finish your tea, eat and be on your way," Lizette said. "Danielle and I will be fine without you."

Danielle and Lizette exchanged amused glances at the relief expressed on Edward's face. "I'm to meet Jameson. I doona wish to be late."

"By all means, go," Lizette said.

Edward swallowed the rest of his tea in one gulp, grabbing a sweet cake before heading for the door.

"Will we see you later?" Danielle asked.

"I don't think so. I'll be quite busy." And off he went.

"He is sweet, but I pity any woman who has to put up with him," Danielle said.

"Tell me how you know Jameson." Lizette poured them both more tea.

How to explain this without leaving room for lots of questions. "Well, I was on my way to Bermuda with some friends when a storm hit and I fell overboard. Jameson happened to be nearby and his crew saved me." It hadn't been a storm in the sense that there was rain and wind, but it was the only thing she could think to call it.

"What happened to your friends?" Lizette asked.

"I don't know." It wasn't a lie. She really had no idea what happened to them and the thought of it made her sad.

"I'm so sorry." Lizette reached out to pat her hand. "I'm sure Jameson has taken good care of you."

Danielle's lips barely turned up in an attempt at a smile.

"I can see it's painful for you to speak of. Jameson is my husband's nephew, you know."

"Jameson mentioned it to me."

"You should know that Jameson will help you in any way that he can, as will my husband and I."

What could she say to that? The kindness she'd experienced since being in this time was so much more than she could have ever hoped for. It was also something she would need a lot more of if she couldn't leave. Conflicting emotions raged through her head. One thing was certain, she hadn't been this troubled by anything in a very long time.

As Jameson approached Red Legs Tavern, he saw a familiar face approaching. "Uncle!"

"Jameson! 'Tis been far too long." Rourke greeted him with a bear hug. "Ye look well."

"I am well."

"Yer visits are always welcome. What brings ye here this time?" Rourke asked loosening his grip on Jameson's shoulders.

"I need the sage advice only an uncle can offer."

"And ye were hoping to find it at Red Legs?"

Jameson laughed. "I couldn't go to the house just yet."

"Let's go inside then and ye can tell me all about it."

Red Legs Tavern was a loud and raucous place frequented more by pirates than the gentle folk of the island.

"Govna'!" The men said in unison when they saw Rourke enter.

He held up a hand in greeting. The barman cleared a table for them to sit and it wasn't long before two tankards of ale were set down before them.

"What troubles ye, son?" Rourke asked.

Jameson took a long pull of his ale, not sure where to begin. He had one big problem and her name was Danielle. "A woman."

"Do ye love her?" Rourke asked, lifting his tankard to drink.

"I believe I do." It was best that he was honest with his uncle.

Rourke placed his tankard on the table. "Does she love ye?"

"She says she does." Jameson tapped the tabletop with his fingers.

"Then all should be well, but I ken love can be a complicated matter and my guess is that things are no' well with ye."

"This would sound strange to anyone else, but in our family perhaps no'." He paused before continuing. He was assuming Rourke would believe him, but could he be sure? He decided he would take his chances. "Danielle is no' from this time." He waited for a reaction, but other than a raised eyebrow, nothing came. "She wishes to return to her own time in the future."

Rourke wrapped his hands around his tankard. "Can she go back?"

"I doona ken if 'tis even possible, but the fact that she wants to leaves me wondering if she'd ever be happy here with me."

"Have ye asked her?" his uncle asked.

"I haven't. I've been too angry."

"That is what ye must do then. Set yer anger aside and speak with her. Yer heart will tell ye what to do."

"I doona believe I can trust my heart. I want Danielle more than I've ever wanted anything. When she said she wanted to go, it was like a knife to my heart."

"Where is she now?"

"She's at yer home with Lizette and Edward."

"Ye left her alone with Edward?" Rourke's eyebrows shot up as his voice was raised in surprise.

Jameson couldn't help but laugh at the picture his uncle presented. "Doona worry. She can handle Edward."

"So can Lizette. Between the two, the man does no' stand a chance." Rourke glanced up as there was movement at the door. "Speak of the devil."

"There ye are," Edward said. "I love yer women, but I'd much rather be here. Another tankard of ale if ye please." He found a chair and joined them at the table.

"How is Danielle?" Jameson asked.

"Confused." Edward leaned on the table, glancing around the room.

"What did she say?" Jameson wasn't sure he wanted to know, but it seemed he had no control over the words leaving his mouth.

"She asked where ye were. I told her ye had business in town. I believe she feels abandoned by ye."

"Abandoned. I've saved the lass no' once or twice, but three times. I'll no' save her again."

"So ye say." Edward winked at Rourke and explained. "I've no' seen the man so in love before."

"Did things go smoothly with Lizette?" Jameson asked his uncle.

"No' at first, but I knew I would do whatever it took to have her in my life."

"Ye gave up *The Dagger*." Jameson understood, because if Danielle wanted him as much as he wanted her, he would do anything for her - even give up his ship for a life on land.

"Lizette would never have asked me to, but I was offered the governorship of Manta Cay. It was time for me to be a more settled man."

"I could never give up my freedom." Edward finished his ale and signaled the barkeep for another.

"Ye will when the right woman comes along." Rourke raised three fingers high in the air for the man serving drinks to see. "Three more."

"There are so many to choose from. I don't believe I would." Edward seemed to get lost in his own thoughts as he rubbed his chin and gazed towards the ceiling.

Three ales arrived at their table and each man took one.

"I'll remind ye of that when ye're all moon-eyed over some lass," Jameson said.

Edward stood, taking his ale with him. "If ye'll excuse me, I see someone I must speak with."

Jameson and Rourke watched as Edward approached Sara, one of the lasses who worked upstairs. She seemed delighted to see him.

"Drink up." Rourke motioned to Jameson's ale as he drained his own tankard. "We should be getting home."

If he hadn't run into Rourke, Jameson would have been happy to stay where he was and to avoid any more contact with Danielle. Being near her every day had tried every ounce of restraint he had. He wanted nothing more than to take her in his arms and hold her close, but instead he'd turned into an ogre. Gruff and moody around her, he found it easier to push her away than to deal with the thought that she didn't love him enough to stay with him. "One more?" he asked.

Rourke pulled him up from his seat, throwing an arm around his shoulders. "I have faith ye can make the lass love ye and convince her to stay. Shall we go try?"

There was no arguing with Rourke when he made up his mind about something. Jameson allowed himself to be pushed toward the door and out onto the street.

"We'll walk. 'Twill give ye time to think of what ye might wish to tell the lass." Rourke gave him a playful shake as they got started.

"How far is it to yer home?" Jameson knew the answer to his own question. "I think I might need to walk around the island a time or two first."

As they headed away from Red Legs and past the docks, Rourke was greeted by every person they passed. He was a well-loved governor. He'd been able to do with Manta Cay what no other island had. Pirates and those who called the island home were able to co-exist with little trouble. Jameson admired him and hoped he could be as good a man someday. If he had Danielle by his side he had no doubt he could be.

CHAPTER 15

Returning to Rourke's home, Jameson saw all the familiar faces he knew from past visits. Guyton was always the first to greet him.

"'Tis good to see you again, sir."

"And ye, Guyton." Jameson said. "Has my uncle been treating ye well?"

"He has. I have been given a much more important role in the household."

Jameson looked to Rourke for more details.

"Guyton is my right-hand man. I depend on him for his counsel and his knowledge of the island."

"I hope ye've fattened his purse." Jameson cocked an eyebrow in Guyton's direction.

"Mightily," Guyton said with a smile and a wink.

"Lizzie!" Jameson kissed his aunt's cheek as she joined them.

"You're looking handsome as ever," she said, smiling sweetly.

"'Tis the good Mackall's blood," Rourke stated.

"Aye, ye speak the truth," Jameson said.

Lizzie laughed. "The two of you make quite the pair."

"Where is the lovely Danielle? I'd like to meet her." Rourke glanced around for her.

"She's in the garden, but I think you can wait. There's someone else she'd rather see."

"Go, lad. Speak with her." Rourke pushed him toward the rear of the house.

Jameson hesitated. He knew it was the right thing to do, but he doubted Danielle would be receptive to what he had to say. He turned back to see Rourke shooing him out.

Passing through the kitchen on his way to the garden, he saw Maria. He stopped to give her a hug and a peck on the cheek.

"Where have you been? I've not seen you in some time. Handsome as ever, I see." Maria smiled brightly as she looked him over.

He smiled just as brightly back in her direction. Maria was a very motherly figure to everyone in the household. "I've been aboard *The Dagger*. I've missed ye and yer good cooking."

"I'll make a special meal tonight. All your favorites," she promised.

"Yer too good to me. I'm a verra lucky man."

"The lass is in the garden. Perhaps you can bring a smile to her face. She seems sad." She pointed to the doorway with her cooking spoon in hand.

"Does she?" He hadn't stopped to think about how Danielle might be feeling. All he knew was that he was hurt and he'd blocked out any sense of what an emotional toll this had been on her. From the very beginning, she'd given the impression that she was a strong lass. She'd survived floating in the sea for hours, she'd handled Domnhaill MacCreary with little trouble and she'd accepted the fact that she may not be able to return home. All of that led Jameson to believe that leaving him would be easy for her. He may have been mistaken.

The garden was in full bloom. Green trees, colorful roses and flowers of all kinds were everywhere. The sweet sound of songbirds made it a peaceful place where one could go to be alone with their thoughts. It was exactly what Danielle was doing as he approached. He hated to disturb her, but as his uncle had told him, he must speak with her. He must tell her he would still be there for her. He'd help her in any way he could.

Danielle glanced up and his heart was happy at the sight of her. She, however, seemed pensive and sad. The beautiful smile he loved failed to appear when she gazed at him.

He continued walking toward her even though it would have been easier to return to the house.

"May I?" he asked, approaching her.

She made room for him on the stone bench where she was seated.

"I want to apologize to ye for no' being the friend ye need. I only thought of myself and for that I am sorry. I pray ye can forgive me." He hoped she could see that he meant every word he was saying.

A single tear slid down her cheek and he wiped it away with his thumb. He hadn't seen her cry. Not once since he'd met her. It hurt his heart.

"I understand if ye doona wish to speak with me. I can leave ye alone if ye wish." He moved to leave.

Danielle gazed at him, eyes filled with sadness. "Please stay."

He was relieved she still wished to be near him.

"I'm sorry, too. I've only been thinking of myself."

"Ye wish to go home. I understand."

"I don't think you do. I don't know how this time travel thing works. I could disappear at any time."

"But ye went to see the woman who would help ye."

"I did. I didn't mean for you to hear what you did. There was more to the conversation than that." She looked away for a moment before turning toward him and taking his hand in hers. "I would have spoken with you first. I wanted to tell you what I was thinking and feeling and when you walked out, I knew I'd lost you."

"Ye did no' lose me. I'm right here."

"But you were angry with me."

"Aye. I admit I was, but I've done some thinking and ken my anger was more with myself than with ye." Her pain was evident to him. It reached inside his chest and yanked at his heart. "I will help ye whether ye wish to go or stay. Ken that I will be yer friend now and forever, no matter where ye are."

D anielle was so saddened by all that had happened that she was having a hard time climbing back out of the hole she'd fallen into. This man...the man she couldn't help but love was offering her his friendship after all she'd put him through. She wanted more than his friendship. So much more. This was one of those times when she realized she couldn't have it both ways. She couldn't have his friendship and have him as a lover. It wouldn't be fair to him. She'd already hurt him when he heard her say she was leaving.

"I'm happy you still want to be my friend. Can I give you a hug?"

He pulled her into his arms, holding her close. Her body tingled from head to toe. Danielle knew he felt it too, because he reluctantly pulled away, leaving her feeling untethered and cold despite the heat of the day.

"Do ye wish to stay here? Or will ye come inside with me." He stood and looked down at her.

Danielle smiled up at him. It was a sad smile, but it was the best she could manage. "I'll come with you." She would follow him anywhere. It was so clear to her, when everything else about her situation seemed muddy. He gave her his arm as he'd done so many times before. She didn't hesitate to take it. He was her rock and her anchor. Without him she'd be truly lost.

Rourke and Lizzie looked at them with question, but neither of them asked a single thing, instead focusing on other easier topics.

"How did you enjoy the garden?" Lizzie asked.

"It's a beautiful place to sit. Very peaceful." Danielle turned toward Jameson.

"I love it. Guyton and Maria keep it looking beautiful year round."

"Where is George? I have no' seen him yet." Jameson glanced around as if expecting to see George somewhere nearby.

"He's sketching on the beach with Rory," Lizette said. "George is my young brother. He's ten and two now," she explained to Danielle.

"He's quite a good artist if I remember rightly."

"Come. I'll show you some of his work." Lizette led them into the drawing room and pointed out several framed images of plants and wildlife found on the island.

"It's beautiful!" Danielle was impressed that someone so young had the ability to produce work that showed an unexpected depth of maturity.

"They'll be back soon."

"Or we could go surprise him," Jameson said, indicating Danielle.

"He'd love that." Lizette's face lit up at the suggestion.

"Ye remember how to get there?" Rourke asked.

"I can sail a ship from port to port without getting lost. I believe I can find the beach from here."

"All right then. Be back in time for our evening meal."

"My little Lily will be up from her nap by then, so you'll be able to meet her," Lizette said to Danielle.

"I'm looking forward to it," she replied.

Danielle followed Jameson out the door. They headed down a rocky path that led them among trees, shrubs and singing birds. He took her hand to guide her over places where she might stumble.

As they emerged onto the beach, they passed a small, one-room cottage. Jameson peeked in the window. "He's no' there."

"I think I see them." Danielle pointed down the beach to two boys. One seated and drawing and the other throwing stones into the ocean.

"Ye'll like George," Jameson said.

"I like him already. He's a very talented artist." She smiled, feeling more comfortable with him than she had in days.

"True. He is. George!" he called, waving at the boy.

"Jameson!" He put his paper down and ran towards them straight into Jameson's arms.

"Ye get taller each time I see ye," Jameson said.

"I hope I do. I'm ten and two now."

"And ye. Yer a full grown man." He pointed to the other boy, who Danielle guessed was Rory.

The boy, who looked to be about sixteen or so, waved and continued lobbing rocks into the water.

"Hello, George. My name is Danielle."

"I'm very pleased to meet you," he said, giving her a slight bow, which she found adorable.

"We were admiring your work back at the house. What are you drawing today?" she asked.

He beckoned them to follow him back to his paper and pen. There on the beach was a starfish entangled in some seaweed. The likeness on his art paper was incredible.

"I found it on the beach this morning, but it was already dead."

"It will live on in yer art," Jameson said.

"I hadn't thought of that." He placed his hand on his chin as he contemplated the starfish. When he looked up again, he was smiling.

"How long will you stay?" he asked Jameson.

"I doona ken. Perhaps until ye tire of me."

"That would be never," George said.

"I agree." Rory threw one last stone into the surf before joining them.

"Danielle and I are going to take a walk down the beach. Ye should head back to the house. We'll be back in time for the evening meal."

"Maria will cook something special for you. She always does." George gathered his things and Rory helped him.

"I can hardly wait," Jameson said.

Danielle followed him as he walked down the beach. He stopped and waited for her to join him.

"I want to wade in the surf," she said, kicking off her slippers and hiking her dress up to reveal her bare legs. "I've always loved doing this, but in my time, we wear a lot less clothing."

Jameson gazed at her with scrunchy eyebrows, causing her to laugh.

"I get it. You can't imagine a woman wearing less clothing."

"Oh, but I can." His tone was playful.

This was the Jameson she'd been hoping to see. It brought joy to her hurting heart.

"Are ye going to tell me what ye wear in yer time?" he asked.

"Definitely not big dresses like this. We wear bathing suits."

"Bathing suits?"

"Yes." She picked up a rock and used it to draw in the sand. She drew a female figure wearing a bikini.

Jameson looked both shocked and intrigued by what she'd drawn.

"Ye have worn this?" he asked.

"I have." She was enjoying his reaction.

"I'd like to see that," he said as though challenging her.

"Well, I can't show you because I don't have one."

"'Tis a shame."

"I really don't want to get my dress wet, but I really want to walk in the water."

Jameson removed his shirt and his boots. He rolled his pants up to his knees.

"That's not fair. It's so easy for you."

"What are ye wearing under the dress?" he asked.

"A shift." He wasn't suggesting what she thought, was he?

"That will do. Turn around." He made a spinning motion with his hand.

She did as he instructed and Jameson undid the laces on the back of her dress. Danielle slipped it off and he placed it with his shirt on the dry sand. He averted his eyes from looking directly at her as she splashed into the surf. "This feels so good."

Jameson was still looking down at the sand.

"You can look at me. It's all right." She had her back turned to the surf and was focused on Jameson. A large wave crashed into her. Danielle lost her balance and fell on her bottom into the knee-deep water. Startled at first, her eyes flew open wide before laughter overtook her. Rather than get up, she decided to stay there. The water felt so good. She turned to face the incoming waves, leaning back on her hands as she did. Looking back over her shoulder, she smiled at Jameson.

He walked out to where she sat, standing behind her as if guarding her from being carried out to sea. After a few moments of small waves making their way past, Jameson walked out farther into the surf before diving in and swimming out several yards to float on his back.

Danielle enjoyed admiring him from afar. Shirtless and tanned, his body glowing in the sunlight, she found that no matter what had happened or what would happen, she wanted him. The thought left her breathless. She'd never felt that way about anyone and there was nothing she could do about it.

Moments later, Jameson strode toward her. Water dripped from his body, making him appear as if he were a fantasy character from a superhero movie. He plunked down beside her.

"Why is it that I can no' think of anything but ye?" he asked.

"I don't know. I'm having the same problem with you."

"What shall we do?" Jameson brushed his dripping ebony locks from his face and turned to face her.

"Enjoy each other's company and try not to think too much about the future." It was the only answer she could offer.

His serious expression softened on hearing her words. "I believe I can do that."

"Me too." She smiled, feeling a small sense of happiness. The easiness they'd shared from the very beginning was there once again.

"We should dry off and head back to the house." He stood and offered her his hand.

Danielle accepted it and he hoisted her up. Feeling off balance, she steadied herself with a hand on his chest. Jameson's eyes met hers and she read longing in them. She thought he might kiss her, but instead he took her hand in his and walked out of the surf.

"If we sit on the beach, our clothes should be dry in no time, but they'll be all sandy."

"I've the perfect place to dry off. Come." Jameson led her back down the beach to the small house they'd seen when they emerged from the trees that edged the beach. "My uncle built this for Lizette. When her father died, she thought she might have to live here. They expected the new governor would live in the house they occupy now."

"But Rourke was the new governor?" Danielle was confused about how this all came about.

"Aye. He saved a British merchant ship from another band of pirates. There were men on board who had influence back in England and they chose him as governor of Manta Cay."

"That was lucky." Entering the house, Danielle could see that it was just one room. Windows all around allowed the light in to shine on the only furniture - an armoire and a bed.

Jameson seemed to be reading her mind. "They planned to make it larger, but there was no need. Now it is a little hideaway for them when they wish to be alone."

Feeling like an intruder in this sweet little cottage, Danielle glanced at Jameson. "They won't mind that we're here, will they?"

"Of course they would no'." He went to the armoire and removed something that looked like a gauzy nightgown. "Give me yer shift and put this on. I'll hang it outside to dry. It should no' take long."

As she changed, he rummaged through the armoire and found breeches for himself. He took her shift and went outside with it. When he returned, he had changed his clothing as well. Jameson then took the dress she'd been wearing and his shirt and shook them out to remove any sand they'd picked up as they lay on the beach.

"Thanks for doing that," Danielle said.

"I would no' wish the sand to irritate yer tender skin."

Keeping Jameson in the friend zone was going to be harder than she thought, but she had to remember that the goal was to enjoy each other's company.

"What should we do while we wait for the clothes to dry?"

Jameson searched the room until he found a deck of cards, which he held up for her to see. "What shall we play?"

"Gin!"

"Gin?" Jameson obviously wasn't familiar with the game.

"I'll teach you." Danielle motioned for him to join her. "Best two out of three is the winner."

He sat down on the bed beside her, leaving a space in the middle for the cards. Danielle explained the rules of the game and then dealt the cards. Jameson picked it up quickly and much to his delight, he won almost every hand.

"I win!" Jameson's face lit up as he spoke. "What is my prize?"

"We're awarding prizes now?" Danielle laughed. "I don't have any money."

"I will accept a kiss as my prize."

"That could be dangerous."

"A kiss between friends. No' dangerous at all."

Danielle thought otherwise and she was sure Jameson knew he was playing with fire. "All right."

She moved the cards out of the way and got closer, anticipating the rush of adrenaline that was about to overtake her as Jameson's lips descended on hers. The room spun as he held her face in his hands. Danielle's hands caressed his still bare chest. She'd been admiring it all afternoon. Her hands moved down to his belly, but before they could go any further the kiss ended. Jameson held her chin in his hand and looked into her eyes with desire flaring in his own.

"Our clothes should be dry," he said, moving away from her and standing.

A half-smile lit her lips as she realized what he was doing. He wanted her to want him. He thought teasing her with a kiss would leave her ravenous for more and he was one hundred percent correct. He had that kind of power over her. She couldn't deny it.

He gathered their things and came back inside handing her the shift and laying her dress on the bed. He turned his back to her, giving her a view of a perfectly sculpted derriere as he exchanged one pair of breeches for another.

Danielle fumbled with her clothes until she finally had donned her dress. Jameson came around behind her and, brushing her hair aside, began lacing the back of the garment. Each time his hands touched her bare skin or his breath tickled her neck, a jolt of desire sparked in her core. By the time he was done, her knees were weak and her insides were quivering with wanting him.

"They'll be expecting us back at the house," he said. A devilish grin curled his lips in a most enticing way.

"Don't think I don't know what you're up to," Danielle said.

"I doona ken yer meaning, lass." He took her hand and they began the torturous walk back. He wasn't making this easy on her. Every brush of his arm on hers, every time he held her hand to help her over a tree root or rock, his smile as he glanced her way were all making this the longest walk of her life.

CHAPTER 16

The table was set with beautiful dishes and silverware. A candles were set in the center of the table and others around the room giving it a romantic feel. The children had eaten and were in their rooms for the night. Danielle had finally gotten to meet little Lily, who was the image of her mother and a very sweet little girl. She glanced around the table and couldn't help but feel at home with this family.

"You were gone quite a while," Lizette said, taking a sip of wine.

"We walked along the beach," Jameson said. "Our clothes were wet, so we stopped in the beach house to dry them."

"How did ye pass the time?" Rourke asked.

"Rourke!" Lizette objected.

"We played cards," Jameson answered.

"Cards. Lizette and I have played many a game of cards in that verra house." Rourke seemed quite amused as he spoke.

Jameson couldn't be sure, but he thought Lizette might have kicked Rourke under the table, because he grimaced and looked toward her.

"My apologies, love," Rourke said.

Lizette, for her part, smiled sweetly at his uncle. He admired their love for one another and had hoped that one day he would find the same. In fact, he thought he had, but unless he could change Danielle's mind, it wasn't meant to be.

"How long have ye lived in New York?" Rourke asked.

"My whole life."

"Yer family lives there?"

"They did." She hadn't had this many questions about her family in ages. Everyone back home knew she had no family. It was strange dredging up memories from her past that she'd worked so hard to keep buried.

"Danielle has no living family," Jameson offered. From his seat across the table he gave her a sympathetic look.

"I'm so sorry," Rourke said. "I did no' mean to pry."

"They've been gone a long time, but it still makes me sad to think of them. I miss them." It was as simple as that. "I have my friends though."

"'Tis good ye've someone." Rourke eyed Jameson.

"Yes. And Jameson has been a good friend to me as well." She smiled warmly at the man seated across from her.

"I wouldn't expect anything less of him," Lizette said.

The dishes were cleared from the table and everyone stood. Rourke and Jameson headed for the drawing room, but before Danielle could join them, Lizette stopped her.

"I like to take a walk in the garden in the evening. Will you join me?"

They went out through the kitchen, and Danielle stopped to compliment Maria on her cooking. Guyton was at her side, helping her with the cleanup. Based on the way they were speaking to each other in whispers and exchanging the kind of looks shared by those in love, she wondered if they were married.

The garden was lit with torches here and there. They gave the perfect amount of light for a stroll along the path. Lizette stopped to pluck a rose from a bush overflowing with pale pink blossoms. She held it to her nose and inhaled deeply before handing it to Danielle. "I love these roses. My father planted them here in memory of my mother. They were her favorite and now they are mine."

The sweet aroma wafted to her nose. "Delicious! You should bottle the scent."

"I do. I make rose water with the petals. If you like, I can show you how." She plucked another rose and twirled it in her fingers.

"I'd love that."

"Tomorrow," she said. "Maria will have the kitchen all cleaned and would not appreciate it if we made a mess tonight."

"Tomorrow it is. I'm excited to learn." She took another sniff of the potent rose scent.

"It's so easy. You'll love it and you'll know how to make your own." Lizette moved on down the path as she spoke. "Tell me about Jameson. What is going on between the two of you?"

"A lot and yet nothing at all." What could Danielle say? It was the truth.

Lizette continued picking roses as they went. She carried a shallow basket hung over her arm and a pair of shears tucked in an apron she'd donned once in the garden. "Do you love him?"

That was a very straightforward question and one there was a definite answer for. "I do, but it's complicated."

"Love is always more complicated than we'd like, but once it takes hold the complications melt away."

"Do you really believe that?" Danielle asked. She could use some good advice on the topic.

"I'm living proof." The glow of the torches showed a sweet smile on Lizette's face.

"Your relationship with Rourke was complicated then?" Danielle asked. They seemed the perfect couple.

"Very. I thought he'd killed my father."

"Oh! That would make things difficult."

"He didn't, of course, but it set us off on an adventure that required both of us to learn the fine art of compromise."

"Obviously it worked, because the two of you are the ideal couple." Danielle had noticed through their interactions that they understood each other completely. With a look or a smile, they communicated so much.

"Jameson is in love with you. I can see it in the way he looks at you."

Danielle knew it was true, but it was nice to have someone else confirm it to her. "Do you really think so?"

"He is completely lost to you," Lizette assured her.

"I'm afraid I might hurt him when I have to leave."

"Then do not go. If you love him as you say you do, there are many gifts you will receive over the years. Will it not hurt you as well to leave him?"

"The thought of it is almost too much to bear, but I don't know if I can stay."

"Why not?"

"It's not something I feel comfortable talking about." Telling Lizette she was from the future may be pushing things. It was best that it was left unsaid.

"I understand. I believe I have enough roses. Let's go inside and put them in water. In the morning we'll have a lesson."

Guyton was waiting for them inside. "The governor and Captain Mackall went into town. He wanted me to let you know he'll be back later."

"Thank you, Guyton."

"I'll take those." He took the roses from Lizette.

"If you'd like to stay up to talk, I'll sit with you," Lizette offered.

"I thought I'd go upstairs to bed."

"I'll come up with you. There are books in my father's study if you'd like something to read."

"I'd like that and a perhaps some paper and something to write with if you can spare it."

"Of course." Lizette headed upstairs and Danielle followed along behind her. She had some things she wanted to jot down about her adventures in the eighteenth century. Perhaps she'd write a book if she ever got back home.

"I call it my father's study, but it's Rourke's now."

"Hopefully Rourke doesn't mind?"

"Not at all. He understands that I miss my father. I loved him dearly."

"I was so sorry to hear about what happened to him."

"It was tragic and I don't imagine he ever expected that his dealings with the pirates of Manta Cay would end that way."

"Are you and Rourke safe?" Danielle was concerned for them.

"Rourke is well respected by everyone on the island. He understands the workings of our pirate community and he keeps our lives completely separated."

"No more pirating for him."

"He's a keen eye for any danger and knows how to handle it. My father didn't."

The study was really more of a library. The walls were covered all around by shelves lined with books. Interspersed here and there were framed pieces of George's artwork. "Your brother is a very talented artist."

"He has been since he was a young lad. His favorite subjects are found on the beach."

"When we saw him earlier, he was sketching a beautiful starfish." Danielle scanned the shelves. She could be happy here for many, many months. Her eyes settled on a book by John Milton called *Paradise Lost.* "I was supposed to read this in school, but I never did."

"You attended school? Where?" Lizette's interest seemed piqued by Danielle's announcement.

"In New York." She forgot that in this time not many women spent time in school and reading books by Milton. "A small school near my home." She clutched the book close to her breast.

"It is just the first book." Lizette pointed to the book Danielle held.

"I didn't realize there were more."

"I believe there are twelve in total."

Twelve. Why hadn't she known that? "I'll just start with this one."

Lizette found some paper, a quill and ink. "There is a small desk in your room. You can write there." She handed the supplies to Danielle, who added the paper to the book she held and took the pen and ink in her other hand.

"Thank you. You've been so kind."

"I love having another woman around the house."

"You have Maria, don't you?" Danielle asked.

"Maria is a second mother to me. I love her dearly."

"Is she married to Guyton?" she asked, having noticed them in the kitchen.

Lizette laughed. "They should be married, but they are not. He dotes on her and though I'm sure she understands his feelings for her I think she prefers the courtship."

"What do you suppose Rourke and Jameson are doing?" Danielle tried to be as nonchalant as possible with her question, but Lizette seemed to see right through her.

"I'm sure Rourke had some business in town and Jameson is keeping him company. Don't worry. They will return unharmed."

Danielle didn't realize how much worry came with being in love with a pirate. She was well aware now that she'd had time to think about it. "How did you convince Rourke to give up life on the sea?"

"It was his choice all along. I would never have asked him to give it up for me, but when the opportunity arose to become governor, he didn't think twice."

Luckily for Jameson, he wouldn't have to make that choice for Danielle. He was free to live his life as he wished, but that didn't mean she wouldn't worry about him.

The wharf area was teeming with men. Some working and some enjoying a night in Manta Cay. Singing could be heard coming from the ships docked in port and as they walked the main street in front of Red Legs Tavern.

"How long will ye stay?" Rourke asked. "I could use a good man here on the island."

"I must take Danielle back to Bermuda," he said, but he had other concerns as well. "I worry that the men will become unhappy with me as their captain."

"Why do ye say that?" Rourke asked.

"We've not found treasure in some time. The Spanish ship we sought has been evasive and the treasure belonging to MacCreary has yet to be found. And then, of course, there's Christopher Plumb's treasure."

"They'll give ye time." Rourke knew the men of *The Dagger* well, having once been their captain.

"Time to ferry a woman back and forth from island to island?"

"Speak with Hawes and Lynk. They'll understand the mood of the men. In the meantime, I've made ye an offer."

"I appreciate it. Lady Charlotte would like me to stay in Bermuda if I were to give up my life at sea."

"Are ye ready?" Rourke glanced over at him awaiting his answer.

Jameson had to give it some thought. "There are times when I think it would be easier to give it up, but I've no reason to do so."

"What of Danielle?"

"She does no' wish to stay with me." It was the sad truth, but the truth nonetheless.

"Surely ye could convince her. Ye're a Mackall!" Rourke shouted.

Jameson chuckled at this. "Do ye believe the Mackall men are gifted with a charm women can no' resist?"

"I do. Lizette finds me irresistible." He winked at Jameson and continued walking.

"Where are we going?"

"I've a man to meet near the beach on the far side of town."

Jameson wondered what on earth he could be meeting this man for in the dark of night. "Do ye no' have meetings in the daylight?"

Rourke laughed. "Aye. 'Tis a special meeting."

They walked on, getting farther and farther away from the noise and bustle of the wharf area. Jameson's intuition told him there was reason to be concerned. He placed one hand on the hilt of his sword and the other on his flintlock pistol. He would be ready to defend his uncle no matter the circumstance.

Shadowy figures lurked beneath the fronds of the palm trees up ahead.

"Is that yer meeting?" Jameson asked.

"Aye. `Tis." He smiled and picked up his pace.

"Rourke, be careful," Jameson warned.

"Pargo!" Jameson approached the men with little or no care for his own welfare.

"Mackall! It's good to see you, my friend," the man said.

This was the notorious pirate Pargo. Jameson had heard much about him, but nothing could surprise him more than his uncle being friends with him.

"This is my nephew, Jameson Mackall. The new captain of *The Dagger.*"

"Good to meet you," Pargo extended a hand, which Jameson shook.

"And ye."

The other man with Pargo seemed to be fulfilling the same role as Jameson. He said nothing and there were no introductions.

"What news have ye?" Rourke asked.

"There are English warships nearby. They seek one of the ships in your harbor."

"Which ship?" Rourke asked.

"*The Serpent.* Finding the ship here in Manta Cay would cause you trouble."

"'Twould be best if they did no' find them here then," Rourke agreed.

"They must leave," Pargo said.

"Will ye be staying in town?"

"Not this time, my friend. I will be back once I find the treasure I seek."

"Thank ye for the information. I'll take care of it right away."

Pargo and his man disappeared into the darkness.

Jameson turned to Rourke. "Do ye no' believe 'twill be to his advantage to have *The Serpent* out on the open ocean to draw attention away from his ship."

"I doona doubt it, but he is right. I can no' risk losing the island. He has done us both a service."

They returned to the wharf area in search of *The Serpent*. Upon finding it, Jameson and Rourke found some of the ship's crew nearby. "Where's yer captain?" Rourke asked.

"Aboard the ship." The man dismissively inclined his head towards *The Serpent*.

"Would ye inform him the governor wishes to speak with him?" Rourke asked.

"Ye can do it yerself," the man said, turning away.

Jameson grabbed the man's arm and yanked him back around. "The governor is speaking with ye. I suggest ye tell yer captain the governor is here."

The man pulled his arm free and snarled at Jameson, but walked back to the ship. They kept an eye on him as he boarded.

"Do ye ken this ship?" Jameson asked.

"This is the first time the ship has docked here while I've been governor."

Minutes passed before the man yelled over the side. "Cap'n says ye can board."

"I'll cover ye," Jameson said as they climbed aboard.

"This way." The man eyed Jameson, the same snarl on his face.

Rourke lowered his voice and spoke close to Jameson's ear. "Watch out for that one."

The Serpent's captain emerged from his cabin and joined them on deck. "What do ye want?"

"I'm Governor Rourke Mackall."

"And?" He appeared unimpressed to have such a distinguished visitor.

"I've been told yer ship is being sought by the English. They're a day or two out from here."

"Who told ye that?" the captain asked.

"A friend who would ken," Rourke answered.

"And why should I believe ye?"

"Ye can take yer chances and stay here, but ye'd be trapped in the harbor. On the open sea ye stand a better chance of evading them."

The captain examined Rourke for a moment. "What's in it for ye?"

"I doona want the English in my harbor. There are a number of ships here that would be at risk, no' to mention my governorship. It would no longer be a friendly port of call."

The man turned and shouted. "Gather the men. We're leaving. If they're no' back within the hour we'll leave without them."

Ignoring Rourke and Jameson, he walked off toward his cabin.

"That was interesting," Rourke said.

"At least he's going without trouble." Jameson walked alongside his uncle. Shoved from behind, his sword was drawn and at the ready as he turned to face the man he'd tussled with earlier. A gun was pointed at his midsection.

Before the man could fire his weapon, Jameson sidestepped him and throwing all his weight behind his sword, he knocked the gun from his hand. As it flew across the deck, the man reached for his sword, but Jameson's blade was at his chest.

Rourke drew his own sword. "Ye put yer life in peril should ye choose to engage with my nephew either by sword or flintlock."

The man glared at them, but put his hands in the air and backed away. Jameson and Rourke headed to the ship's gangplank, keeping their weapons in hand. Once clear of the wharf, they sheathed their swords and made their way back home.

"I believe ye made the man angry," Rourke laughed, before eyeing Jameson with obvious concern. "Ye were lucky the man did no' shoot ye in the back."

"I should be grateful that the man had some scruples, I suppose."

They walked on in silence. Jameson's only thought was of Danielle. If anything happened to him, he wasn't sure who would aid her in her quest to return to her own time.

CHAPTER 17

The next morning, Danielle was up early to have her lesson on making rose water. Lizette was watching Lily, who was seated on the floor of the kitchen playing with a small doll. The child chatted happily to it, which brought a smile to Danielle's face. It was just after sunup and no one else in the house was awake. Maria and Guyton were the exception and they were working in the garden, so the ladies had the kitchen to themselves. Lizette heated a bucket of rainwater she'd retrieved from the rain barrel just outside the kitchen door. Danielle plucked the petals from the roses being careful not to prick herself with the thorns. Lizette then placed the petals and rain water in a large pot, setting it on a hook over the kitchen fire. The petals simmered away until their color began to fade and their aroma filled the kitchen with the most delightful scent.

"They are done." Lizette carefully moved the pot from the fire to the table. She handed Danielle a wooden spoon. "To remove the petals."

Danielle was surprised how easy it was. "Is this all we have to do?" She carefully used the spoon to remove the petals and set them aside.

Lizette nodded her head as she began filling bottle after bottle with the water. After little more than an hour from start to finish,

Lizette placed a cork in the top of the last bottle and handed it to Danielle. "This one's for you."

"Are you sure?" Danielle held the beautiful, yet simple, bottle up where the light streaming in through the window changed the color of the bottle from a deep sapphire blue to a lighter shade.

Gathering up the rest of the bottles and placing them in a basket, Lizette stood back and seemed to admire their work. "Of course. You worked just as hard to make it as did I."

Danielle was touched by this woman she hardly knew. Lizette had welcomed her into her home and made her feel comfortable, as if she were one of the family. "I'll treasure it."

"Now you know how to make it yourself and will be able to do so no matter where you are…as long as you have roses." Her smile was infectious. "Go put it with your things and then come back down for some breakfast."

Danielle glanced down to see Lily was still busy with her doll. "She's been so good."

"She's a good little one. I'm very lucky to be her mother."

Brushing her fingers through Lily's hair, Danielle wondered what it would be like to have a child of her own. It hadn't been something she'd given much thought to back in New York, but here the thought seemed appealing to her. She headed up the stairs to her room, but before she could get there, Jameson appeared from the room next to hers.

"Good morn to ye." He finished putting his shirt on and began buttoning it. "What have ye there?"

"Rose water. Lizette and I made it this morning. She gave me this beautiful bottle." Danielle held it up to his nose.

"Will ye wear it?" he asked after sniffing at the bottle.

"I'm pretty sure I will."

"Then I look forward to smelling it on ye." Jameson brushed past her and jogged down the stairs.

Danielle was left watching him go. The very sight of him gave her a tingling sensation from head to toe. Damn him. Why did he have to be so darn appealing to her?

When she returned to the dining room, Jameson was already eating. Food had been set out on the sideboard and she helped herself before joining him.

Jameson put eggs on his fork, glancing up at her before placing it in his mouth.

"I know what you're doing." Danielle leaned on the table, setting her chin in her hand as she gazed at him.

"Aye. Yer most observant. As ye can see, I'm eating." One side of his lip curled into the most alluring half smile.

Danielle pursed her lips, sitting back up in her chair and wondering when it was exactly that she'd lost her ability to resist him.

"We leave for Bermuda today." Jameson sipped his tea.

Danielle was surprised to hear this. "So soon?"

"Ye want to go home and my men would like to get back to the work of finding treasure."

It was a very matter-of-fact statement. One that confused Danielle. Yes, she wanted to go home, but she was enjoying her time on Manta Cay. "So you're trying to get rid of me?"

"'Tis no' what I said. Ye take my words and twist them." He continued smiling at her with what was now becoming an annoying smirk.

Her fork was poised in her hand with a small bit of egg that had been sitting there through their conversation. "I was hoping we would stay at least a few more days."

"'Tis no' possible."

She didn't wish to be a burden to anyone and if he was that anxious to see her gone, then her departure couldn't come soon enough.

He stood, wiped his mouth with the napkin he was holding and walked past her to the door of the dining room. "When ye've finished yer meal we'll say our goodbyes and be on our way."

She put her hand to her head in a salute. "Aye, aye, captain." What was happening? She thought things were better between them and now he was making it seem that he couldn't wait to be rid of her.

ameson climbed the stairs to his room where he gathered his things. He had sparked an interesting response from her. Perhaps she wasn't as eager to leave as she'd led him to believe. The next four days aboard *The Dagger* would be the deciding factor. She would either end the trip more in love with him than she had been or she would be on her way home. He would have to reconcile his feelings, if she chose the latter.

He checked the room one last time before heading back downstairs to speak with Rourke.

"Are ye sure ye wish to leave today?" Rourke opened the front door and bid Jameson to follow him outside. "We can speak privately here."

"Aye. I can no' continue to wait for Danielle to change her mind. I must force the issue."

"I hope yer plan works."

"As do I."

"Remember my offer. If ye decide ye've had enough of the seafaring life, I can always use a good man here on the island."

"I won't forget." He looked out toward the road that would lead him away from his uncle's home. "I've sent word to the men to be ready to depart. They'll be waiting."

The door opened and Danielle and Lizette appeared along with George, Rory and Lily.

"You're out here," Danielle noted. "Someone's in a hurry to be gone."

"Lizette, it has been a pleasure to visit with ye. I'll be back again soon," Jameson said.

"I hope so, Jameson. You're always welcome here and you can stay as long as you like."

"I have wasted too much time sailing from island to island. I've a ship full of men that expect more of me."

"I understand." Lizette hugged him and went to stand by Rourke, who placed an arm around her shoulders.

"I wish I did," Danielle muttered.

Jameson heard her, but he wanted her to say it out loud. "Did ye say something, lass?"

"Just that we should be on our way." She hugged Lizette and then Rourke. "I don't know if I'll ever see you again, but I want you to know how happy I am to have met you. You've been so kind. I'll never forget it."

Jameson hugged George before picking Lily up. He kissed her cheek and gazed lovingly at her. "Doona grow too much before I see ye again."

Lily giggled and put her finger on the tip of his nose before he handed her over to Rourke.

"Rory, I'll see ye soon, lad."

"Aye, Cap'n." Rory waved. At sixteen he was reluctant to hug Jameson, which was not unexpected.

Jameson held out his arm for Danielle to take, but she didn't seem interested in accepting it. Instead, she waved to their hosts and marched past him toward the road.

Jameson raised his eyebrows as he looked back to see Rourke and Lizette appearing quite amused by the situation.

"Ye'd best hurry." Rourke chuckled. It was apparent he thought it funny that Danielle had turned the tables on him.

Jameson caught up with Danielle easily as she carefully avoided the ruts and rocks that created obstacles in her path.

"Let me help ye." He tried to take her arm, but she stopped and glared at him. "Ye're angry."

"No, I'm not." She turned away from him and continued on.

"I would disagree with ye, but I can see that would only make ye angrier than ye already are."

Her feet were flying along the path, but Jameson's long stride was able to keep up with her. He was ready to catch her if she fell into a hole along their route. It would also give him a chance to relish the feel of her in his arms once again. He knew it was wrong to hope she turned her ankle, but the thought of carrying her all the way to *The Dagger* would alleviate some of his guilt.

The skiff was awaiting them on the beach by the docks. Jameson offered Danielle his hand as she boarded, but she ignored him.

Hawes did the same and she accepted. "Did ye enjoy yer time on Manta Cay?"

"I did. I wish I didn't have to leave," she said, giving Jameson an angry glare.

"I'm sure the Mackalls would've been happy to have ye." Hawes sat and took up the oars. Lynk, Samuel and Owen joined him as they made their way back to *The Dagger*.

"It seems I must go back to Bermuda. I've kept you all from whatever it is you do every day."

Hawes' questioning face looked back at Jameson who'd seated himself behind Danielle. Instead of acknowledging him, he focused on the fact that they seemed to be taking a very long time to get back to their ship. "Can ye row any faster, lads? There are English warships approaching the island."

"Aye, Cap'n." All three men picked up the pace, moving the skiff along at a good clip.

The rope ladder was dropped as they approached. Hawes held out his hand for Danielle, helping her get a hand and foothold before proceeding upwards.

"Sir?" Hawes waited for Jameson.

He glanced up at Danielle who seemed to be struggling to make it to the top. One of the lads aboard ship reached over the side, but she was obviously afraid to let go and take his hand. Jameson sprinted up the ladder until he was right behind her. "Take his hand. I'll see that ye doona fall."

Thankfully, she did as he said instead of arguing the point and she was on board in no time. Jameson and the rest of the crew boarded and the skiff was taken care of. "Where's Edward?"

"Here!" Edward appeared from below deck. "Is Danielle aboard?"

"Aye." He'd just finished watching her march her way towards his cabin. "Prepare to weigh anchor."

The men all scrambled to do as their captain had ordered, leaving

Jameson standing alone and wondering if he should try to speak with Danielle. Deciding it would be best to let her have some time alone, he checked in with his crew before departure. He was pleased to note they'd restocked their provisions with fresh fruit and vegetables from the island along with anything else they'd run low on. They were a fine crew. He was proud to be their captain. Despite their occasional grumbling, they spent more of their time laughing and singing than complaining. Most ships would do anything to keep a woman from boarding, but these men didn't hold to those old superstitions. They'd welcomed Danielle aboard and despite what he'd told her, they were pleased she was there.

Danielle stomped around the cabin. Jameson Mackall infuriated her. She was furious he obviously wanted to be done with her and she was furious that she was so attracted to him. The thing that made her the angriest was that she was in love with him and thought he was with her, too. The way he'd been acting this morning seemed to say otherwise.

It was times like this that she wished she had her cell phone or computer. She needed Susanna to bounce things off of. She always gave her the best advice. Danielle sat on the edge of the bed, ready to give in to her sadness and confusion when she remembered the pen and paper she'd received from Lizette and the letter she'd started writing to Susanna. She took it out of her bag and read over what she'd said. She wondered if she were actually able to post it if it would someday make its way to Susanna in New York. She'd addressed it properly. All she needed was an envelope. Did they even have those in this time period? She'd have to see. It would be an interesting experiment.

In the letter, she'd told Susanna all about what had happened to her, wondering if the others on the boat had made it to Bermuda and the luxury hotel she'd booked for everyone. Danielle smiled to herself. As soon as they reached Bermuda, she was going to find a way to mail it. Then she'd meet with the woman who held the key to her future.

CHAPTER 18

*H*alfway to Bermuda and Jameson's plan to convince Danielle to stay with him was taking shape. She seemed unaware of his intentions, which was a good thing. He would be her friend, but he knew that with each look, each touch, he was drawing her closer and closer to him. If it worked, she would not leave him. She'd be happy to stay and make a life with him here in this time.

Danielle had ventured out of his cabin a few times, but never for very long. Today she stood by the rail looking out at the vast expanse of ocean in front of them. Various members of his crew passed by her, some giving her a brief nod and others stopping to speak with her. Hawes had a lengthy and very animated conversation with her before going off to attend to his duties. Edward was headed her way when Jameson stopped him.

"I was just going to speak with your lady." Edward was determined to continue on toward Danielle.

"Stop. I wish to speak with the lass." Jameson grabbed his arm, halting him on the spot.

Edward raised his hands in surrender. "As you wish."

Jameson wondered what she was thinking about as he approached her. She didn't seem to realize he was there until he spoke. "'Tis a beautiful day."

A spray of mist blew over them on a gentle gust of wind, and rather than the salty sea air, Jameson smelled roses. "Do ye wear yer rose water?"

"I put some on this morning," she answered, still facing the water.

Jameson gently moved her long golden locks from her neck and dipped his head to take in the scent. His nose barely brushed across her skin as did his fingers. He noted a slight tensing of her neck and shoulders, before they relaxed and she leaned into him. His hands moved to her shoulders. He supported her as she seemed unsteady on her feet.

"Ye should hold onto the rail," he whispered into her ear. Once she had her hands firmly in place, he let go of her and walked away. There was no need for Jameson to turn back to see if she was watching because Edward was waiting and the grin on his face told him everything he needed to know.

"You tease the lass," he said as Jameson approached.

"Aye. Ye read me well." He was quite pleased with himself.

"From the look of her, you could do more than tease." Edward was still peeking over his shoulder at Danielle. "I will speak with her. Shall I put in a good word or two for you?"

"I doona need yer help, but I expect ye to tell me what she says."

"Aye, Cap'n."

Edward headed for Danielle and Jameson smiled to himself before tending to his duties. He was enjoying the pursuit, because the prize he sought was more valuable to him than gold.

The *Dagger* would be arriving in Bermuda the next morning. He'd seriously considered bypassing the port of St. George's altogether and heading to some faraway place where Danielle wouldn't be able to meet with the witch who would surely take her away from him. Instead, he would have faith that his plan would work and that she would decide to stay by his side forever.

Jameson knocked on his cabin door. Something he wasn't used to, but he knew he should give Danielle the opportunity to deny him entrance if she so chose.

"Yes." Danielle was curled up on his bed seeming to be lost in thought.

"May I come in?" he asked.

"It's your cabin." She sat up, tipped her head and looked at him with the saddest eyes. No matter the situation they'd found themselves in, she'd always somehow managed to keep herself in good spirits. Something was troubling her.

He was across the room in two long strides. "What's wrong?" He knelt in front of her, taking her hands in his.

"Nothing you can fix." She glanced down at their hands joined together on her lap.

He was sure he could fix anything and was surprised that she doubted he could. "I doona understand."

"I'm tired."

"Then sleep." It was an easy enough solution.

"Not that kind of tired." She let out an exasperated sigh. "I'm tired of the not knowing. I'm tired of the waiting."

He understood what she was trying to say. She was tired of being here with him. It must have registered on his face because she was quick to add. "It's not you. I don't think I could ever be tired of you."

He lifted her hand to his lips and kissed her palm. A soft smile caressed her lips. "I doona understand yer sadness. If no' me, then what causes ye to be sad?"

"I don't know where I belong anymore. It can't be here in this time, but it may be that I don't belong in my own time either."

"Ye do belong here." Jameson didn't think that was what she wanted to hear, but he wanted her to know it was what he believed to be true.

"I just feel unmoored. Adrift like a ship without a crew to guide her."

He could guide her. He could be her anchor if only she'd have him.

"We'll be in Bermuda soon. I'll see the woman Lady Charlotte sent me to. Maybe she can help me."

Until this very moment, he'd had some hope that she might stay with him, but it was more than apparent that she planned to go back to her home. He couldn't be angry with her. If he had somehow found himself in a similar situation, wouldn't he want to be back where everything was familiar and comforting?

"I'll take ye to her." He heard the words leave his mouth and felt as though he had no control over what he was saying.

"Would you?" She seemed surprised by his offer of help.

"Aye. I would do anything for ye, lass."

"Would you stay with me tonight? I don't want to be alone."

It was an invitation he couldn't turn down.

Danielle placed her hands on his face before kissing him. A long, slow, sensual kiss. She'd turned the tables on him. He'd been trying to make her want him and it was obvious she did, but it was also obvious that she had control of his heart and soul. He was hers to do with as she pleased.

But for the moment, his only intent was to *please her*. He would make her his own one more time before he had to let her go - perhaps forever.

Gazing into her lovely face, all Jameson could think of was being one with her. It was the only way he could show her how he felt and how much she meant to him.

Making sure the cabin door was locked and they would be free from interruption, Jameson undressed. Danielle did the same and waited for him on his bed. A contented sigh escaped her as he took her in his arms. He hoped she could see the love he felt for her and how much she meant to him.

"Jameson..." She tangled her fingers in his hair and nuzzled her nose into his neck.

He turned to face her. She kissed him and it felt like the last time to Jameson.

"I'll never forget you," she said in a breathy whisper.

His heart was breaking. He couldn't lose her, but he also couldn't keep her. "Nor I ye. Ye'll always be in my heart." He placed her hand on his chest and covered it with his own.

Her eyes were brimming with tears that fell from her lashes onto her cheeks. Jameson kissed them away, tasting the saltiness of them. "Doona cry, Danielle. Doona cry." He kissed her eyes, her nose, her lips. He felt helpless for the first time in his life. It seemed there was little he could do to ease her pain, but he would try.

He ran his hand down her side, relishing the soft contours of her shape before pulling her closer. He wanted to feel every part of her body pressed against him. Their legs and feet tangled as he kissed her, pouring every ounce of the love he felt into her. He was overcome with it and he hoped she could feel it and that it would soothe her.

Danielle hung onto him as though her life depended on it. Her hunger for him was apparent as she wrapped one leg over his hip, rubbing herself on his hardened cock.

"I want you," she said, kissing his neck.

"I'm yers." He positioned himself at her entrance before slowly guiding himself into her warmth. Her soft moans were music to his ears as he moved in her. With every thrust, he felt closer and closer to her and to the pinnacle of pleasure he sought.

Danielle's soft whispers of love drove him on until her excitement grew. She writhed beneath him, her back arched, her hands grasping his backside drawing him further in. Bliss and delight were joined by satisfaction as they both reached the explosive ending of their passion-filled coupling and collapsed in each other's arms.

"I love ye, Danielle." Jameson's words were barely audible as he held her close and kissed the top of her head. Losing her was going to be the hardest thing he'd ever had to endure.

CHAPTER 19

As the ship docked in Bermuda, Danielle couldn't help but think about the first time she'd seen this port and her shock on realizing that it wasn't the place she'd expected it to be. She'd only been on this time travel journey a few short weeks, but it felt like a lifetime. It amazed her every time she thought about it. Danielle had made a journey through the veil of time and found a man who was her match in every way. Jameson was exactly what she needed, wanted and had never found. Perhaps it was because the man she was meant to be with couldn't be found in twenty-first-century New York. Instead he was here in the most unlikely of places and times.

Watching Jameson work, shouting orders to his men and seemingly everywhere at once, Danielle took the time to admire him from her position along the rail. He'd surprised her in so many ways and she knew that if she stayed, theirs would be a life filled with joyful and unexpected adventures whether in port or at sea. As he strode across the deck toward her, her belly did that little flip-flop she'd come to expect whenever she thought about him. She wondered if her return to New York would put an end to it.

"Are ye ready?" Jameson was at her side.

The concern etched on his face was apparent. She wanted to ease it for him, but she couldn't. Not until she met with the witch who lived by the beach. "I'm ready."

Danielle wove her arm through his and he led her down the gangplank onto the pier.

"Shall we visit Charlotte first?" he asked.

"I'd like that." Danielle wanted to thank her for everything. For her hospitality and especially for sharing her story with Danielle. Jameson was unaware of the tale Lady Charlotte had told her on their last visit. Maybe it was time for him to find out, but she wouldn't be the one to tell him. Danielle would leave that to Lady Charlotte.

"Edward will see to the ship, so we can take all the time we need."

Danielle glanced around her at the busy docks and then as they approached the street where Lady Charlotte lived, she realized that despite being away from her own home, there was something about this place that eased her mind. She felt at peace here and much more relaxed than she did in New York. "I love this island."

"It has a charm all its own." Jameson gently squeezed her hand as she gazed at him.

Torn by the decision she had to make and unsure if she even had a choice, Danielle clung to Jameson as they walked.

He seemed to realize she needed his strength in that moment because he released her hand and placed a strong arm around her shoulders, bolstering her courage and letting her know he would be there for her. She rested her head on him, not caring what others they passed might think of her. How could she leave this man? How could she stay?

L ady Charlotte waited for them in the drawing room. She stood and accepted a hug from each of them before sitting once again.

"I'm a lucky woman. I've had three visits from you in a short time." Her warm smile was focused on Jameson. "Sit, please."

They did as she instructed, while she rang a bell for tea.

"What brings you back to Bermuda?" she wondered.

Jameson looked to Danielle and then back to Lady Charlotte. "Danielle wishes to meet with the witch."

Danielle seemed uncomfortable discussing this, but it was what they'd come back for. "She wasn't there the last time and things didn't end well."

"I thought you might have made your journey back to your own time, but I stopped in to visit with Morwenna and she told me that she had not seen you."

"I was kidnapped by Domnhaill MacCreary," Danielle explained.

Lady Charlotte's eyebrows shot up in surprise.

Jameson explained everything that had taken place while their tea was being served.

"I'm happy you weren't harmed, Danielle." She held her teacup up as if toasting her.

"Every time I seem to land in trouble, Jameson is there to save me." She gazed lovingly at the man who had rescued her without question, at times putting his life and his ship at risk for her.

"A true hero." Lady Charlotte's obvious affection for Jameson was written all over her face.

"I'm no hero. I'm a pirate." Jameson protested, brushing off her compliment.

"I believe you can be both," Charlotte said.

"I would have to agree," Danielle added.

Jameson was uncomfortable with their praise. Changing the subject seemed a good idea. "It appears a storm is approaching. The sky is dark. It will rain soon."

Charlotte laughed. "You may ignore our comments if you wish."

"I wish," he chuckled. "Danielle, I would like to speak to Charlotte alone, if ye wouldn't mind."

"Not at all," she said. "I think I left some things upstairs. I'll just go check."

As she stood to leave, he took her hand and pressed it to his lips.

"I'll take my time." She smiled as she left the room.

"You love her very much, I can see it."

"I can no' hide it, especially from ye."

"It will be hard to see her go."

"That is why I wished to speak with ye alone."

"I'm listening."

"I've never loved anyone like this. I doona ken what to do or say that may change her mind."

"All you can do is let her see your love. It is a difficult decision she has to make. You can understand, I'm sure."

"I'm trying. I doona wish to be selfish. Her happiness is my only concern."

"There's something you should know. Something I've never shared with you."

"What would that be?"

"Like Danielle, I too found myself in a time where I didn't belong."

Jameson was shocked that he hadn't known this about her. "How is it that ye've never told me?"

"I've kept it to myself all these years. Harold was the only one who knew."

"Were ye able to go back?"

"No. Not until after Harold died. Then I didn't wish to leave."

"I see. Do ye believe Danielle will be able to go?"

"Morwenna will see to it. It's up to Danielle to make the ultimate decision."

"When you first arrived in this time, did you try to go back? Did ye want to?"

"I did want to go back and I tried, but the door was closed to me. I believe it was because I was to fall in love with Harold. Fate had a master plan. It was one I was unaware of. When I couldn't return to my own time, Harold and I had already been falling in love. My disappointment at not being able to go home was tempered by Harold's love and his acceptance of the fact that the choice was mine, not his."

"He didn't ask ye to stay?"

"He did, but he also left it up to me. He knew that if I stayed only because he wanted me to that I might resent him someday and he didn't want that, so he made the decision to let me go."

"But ye couldn't."

"I'm sorry to say that if I had been able to, I wouldn't be sitting here right now."

"Ye are happy ye stayed?"

"Yes. Time was what I needed and it seemed it was on my side."

"Do ye miss Harold?"

"More than I can say. I think of him every day. I stay because I feel close to him here in our home and on this island. My memories are all I have left, but they are all good ones."

Jameson hoped that somehow Danielle would have to stay as Lady Charlotte had been forced to. That the witch wouldn't be able to help her leave him. He wished it with all his heart and soul.

Danielle sat on the bed upstairs wringing her hands in her lap. Why had she been sent to this time? She knew she could stay and there was a very large part of her that wanted to, but she was afraid that if she didn't take this opportunity to go home she would never have another one. Her world seemed to be crumbling around her, but what could she do? Having everything she wanted didn't seem possible. She'd been over these questions time and again and now she was faced with the reality that it would all be over soon.

Jameson wouldn't try to hold her here. She knew he wanted whatever it was that she wanted. If only she knew clearly what that was. Why couldn't she have met him in her own time? So many questions, so few answers. She gathered the few things she had to take with her. Hawes told her that her clothes had been thrown overboard at some point after they'd found them on the floor of the captain's cabin. She was going to have to make this journey dressed in eighteenth-century garb and hope no one asked too many questions when she arrived back in her own century.

Glancing out the window, she saw the storm clouds darkening the sky. If she was going to do this, now was the time. She picked up the things Jameson had bought her on her first day in Bermuda and, holding them close to her heart, went back downstairs.

"I'm ready," she said.

Jameson stood and turned to Charlotte. "I'll be back soon."

"John will be waiting outside with your horse."

Danielle had no idea that Jameson had a horse. "No carriage?" she asked.

"I thought Jameson would want to take you all the way to Morwenna's cottage." Charlotte crossed the room. She hugged Danielle. "No matter what happens, know that you are loved and cared for."

"I will."

Jameson took her hand and they walked out of the little blue house where John waited for them. Jameson helped Danielle up to sit sidesaddle and then hopped up behind her. John handed him the reins and they moved off.

Danielle took one last look at this place and hoped that maybe someday she would see it again.

CHAPTER 20

*J*ameson rode with Danielle seated in front of him. He wrapped his arms around her as they made their way to the small one-room cottage on the beach. When they arrived, Danielle slid down to the ground with a little help from Jameson.

She didn't know what to say. She'd told him how she felt and he'd done the same. She stood on her tiptoes as he leaned down to kiss her goodbye. She grasped his leg as his hand traced her jaw before combing through her hair and holding one long tress between his fingers before letting it drop. He hadn't asked her to stay, but even if he had she wasn't sure she could.

The door to the cottage was open, so there was no worry that the witch wouldn't be there this time.

"I hope you find the treasure you've been searching for."

"I thought I had," he replied.

The knot in her belly grew as her throat ached with unshed tears. She wouldn't cry. She couldn't do that to him. It was obvious Jameson was keeping his emotions in check and that he would let her go without a fight. It was what was best for them both.

He turned the horse and headed away from her at a walk just as the skies opened up and rain began to pour down. Danielle hurried to the doorway, knocking on the open door.

"Come in. I've been waiting for ye," Morwenna said.

She sat at a small table that, along with a bed and two chairs, seemed to be the only furniture. A candle was lit in the center of the table because despite the windows, the room was gloomy and dark.

"I'm Danielle York. I think Lady Charlotte told you about me. I was here once before, but you were out."

"I was away, but it wasn't yer time," Morwenna said.

Danielle wasn't sure what she meant by that. "So, you know why I'm here."

"I do. I'd like to hear ye say it though, if ye doona mind."

"All right." She tried to get her thoughts in order before speaking, but they were all jumbled and she was afraid that was how they would come out.

"I want to go home." There, she'd said it.

"Where is home?" the witch asked, a knowing glint in her eye.

That was a bit tougher to answer. "I'm not sure, but I'm from the New York of the future."

"But ye've a home here as well, aye?"

"I guess you could say that. I don't know what to do. I feel like I should go back to my own time, but I also want to stay here to be with Jameson."

"That is a dilemma." She laid some cards down on the table and mumbled to herself as she gazed at them.

"I can no' tell ye what to do, but I can help ye. I've something that will leave the decision in yer own hands, no' mine."

The woman rose and went to a basket in the corner of the room. She rummaged around in it as if she were searching for something with her hands and definitely not with her eyes. After a few moments, her hand emerged with a strange looking stone. "I'm sorry for the delay. I had to be sure I had the right one for ye." She handed it to Danielle.

Danielle looked at the stone. It was perfectly round and sand-colored like the beach on the bottom with a clear, frosty blue on the top. In the center was what appeared to be a wave. "What am I supposed to do with this?"

The woman held out her hand. "Give it back. I must spell it."

Danielle handed it back and Morwenna took it in her hands again muttering words that were not loud enough for Danielle to hear.

"There. Ye can have it now. If ye turn it in yer hands three times, it will take ye back to yer own time, so be careful."

"So, you mean if I don't want to go just yet, I don't have to." Danielle was surprised at how happy that made her.

"Aye. Ye were meant to be here and ye were meant to arrive when ye did. Did ye no' question why it was only ye that was thrown into the sea?"

"Not really. Does that mean that everyone else on the boat is safe?"

"They all made it home safely if not sadly at yer loss."

Danielle thought about her friend Susanna and wished she could let her know she was alive and well. "I wrote a letter to my friend. If I mail it, will she get it?"

Morwenna seemed taken aback by her question. "Hmmm...let me see." She set out more cards, did more muttering and then gazed up at Danielle. "Aye. She will receive it."

"Thank you. How can I repay you?"

"Doona worry about that. Lady Charlotte has taken care of everything."

Jameson stood outside of the cottage, soaking wet and unsure of what to do. He was always so confident in everything that he did and said, but not when it came to Danielle. He'd gotten about halfway to Charlotte's when he turned his horse and galloped back. The only question now was if he was too late. He had been a fool to let her go. He kicked at the sand with his boots and punched a palm tree with his fist, cutting his knuckles in the process.

He made up his mind and pounded on the door to the cottage. "Danielle! Danielle! Are ye still here?"

The door opened and Danielle stood there staring at him. He had to tell her, had to say what he should have said before leaving her here. "Please doona go. Stay here with me. I love ye." Water dripped from his hair into his eyes and he brushed it away with the back of his hand. It took a moment to register, but Danielle was smiling at him. It wasn't a sad smile, but a bright, joyful smile.

Before he could say another word, she was in his arms. "I'm not going anywhere. I want to be with you. I love you."

Sweeping her up into his arms, he held her close. She clung to him, nestling her head beneath his chin.

"Ye've made me a happy man, Danielle. I vow I will love ye and protect ye all the days of my life."

"Can we go home now?" she asked. "I want to go home with you." Water streamed down her face and dripped from her hair.

"Aye. Ye will no' mind living on my ship?"

"If I'm with you, I can live anywhere."

All of the worries he'd had evaporated as he carried her to his horse and set her atop. He leapt up behind her and wrapped her in his arms. Nudging the horse forward with his legs, they made their way back to Lady Charlotte's.

Hopping down from his horse, he lifted Danielle into his arms and set her on the ground. John was waiting for them and took the horse to the stables.

"What shall we do now?" Jameson asked. He was sure he didn't deserve her, but he would spend the rest of his life trying to prove that he did.

Danielle gazed up at him with love in her eyes. "I've got a few ideas, but first I've got a letter to mail."

A NOTE FROM JENNAE

Thank you so much for reading Green Sky At Night. If you enjoyed Jameson and Danielle's story and have a minute to spare, I would really appreciate a short review on the page or site where you bought the book. Your help in spreading the word is greatly appreciated. Reviews from readers like you make a huge difference in helping new readers find stories similar to Green Sky At Night.

If you'd like to know when my next book comes out and want to receive occasional updates from me, then you can sign up for my newsletter here: https://www.subscribepage.com/w4j6s3

ACKNOWLEDGMENTS

As always, I'd like to thank my editor Reina Williams for all your help. I'd also like to thank Sheri McGathy for the beautiful cover you created for this book and the entire series. Thanks also goes out to you, the reader, for taking a chance on this book. Your support is always appreciated.

ABOUT THE AUTHOR

Jennae Vale is a best selling author of romance with a touch of magic. As a history buff from an early age, Jennae often found herself daydreaming in history class and wondering what it would be like to live in the places and time periods she was learning about. Writing time travel romance has given her an opportunity to take those daydreams and turn them into stories to share with readers everywhere.

Originally from the Boston area, Jennae now lives in the San Francisco Bay area, where some of her characters also reside. When Jennae isn't writing, she enjoys spending time with her family and her pets, and daydreaming, of course.

www.jennaevaleauthor.com

THE THISTLE & HIVE SERIES

A Bridge Through Time

A Thistle Beyond Time

Separated By Time

A Matter of Time

A Turn In Time

All In Good Time

A Long Forgotten Time

Awakened By Time

Saved By Time

In Time For Edna

A Thistle & Hive Christmas

THE MACKALLS OF DUNNET HEAD

Her Trusted Highlander

Her Noble Highlander

Her Mysterious Highlander

THE DELIGHT SERIES

Wanted

Watched

Wounded

Christmas In Delight

THE GREEN SKY SERIES

The Dagger - Prequel

Green Sky At Night

OTHER BOOKS BY JENNAE

A Highlander In Vegas